Soar

By Hannah O'Neal

Chapter 1: Fly or Die

Arne

Think streamlined...focus. Escape, fly harder...

I furiously beat my white wings and fly for dear life. I can hear the wing beats behind me...if I do not gain speed, this will be the end.

No! I think. *I must go faster!* I strain my wings, thinking of every time I've flown, and try to put that into every stroke. I know I have to get away. If not, I will never be able to fly again. And that is an unbearable thought for a bird. Especially for an owl.

The moon stands softly in the darkness of the night, trying to show me the way. I cannot give up. *Fly harder, go faster, anything to get away...fly harder, go faster, and* get away...

My opponent's battle cry splits through my thoughts like an axe through wood. I lose focus, and try to beat harder. I have never flown this hard. Never in my life. I am famed for my silent flight, not my speed. I can feel my shoulder muscles straining and do not know how much time I have.

Living in the Dilecta Arctic, I should be stronger. Even though I am female, I should be strong. Perhaps it was the shock of the sudden attack. No, I've handled winter wolves. I can handle this owl. No problem, right?

The Dilecta Arctic is soon gone below me, and the edges of the Bleian Desert and Worte Marsh quickly rush past. The Arko Forest looms ahead, a giant dark green wall stark against the crystal blue sky.

My feathers being the color of freshly-fallen snow, I am best suited in the arctic tundra or at least snowy areas, where all Snowy owls use their camouflage best. But the Eurasian eagle owl that is now chasing me has driven me away from Dilecta Arctic, for reasons I cannot understand...

I am thinking so hard to make sense of my current situation that I have lost speed. By the time I snap out of it and realize that I've slowed it's too late. I feel her talons like metal death claws dig into my right shoulder. I cry out in almost a scream, but the owl wouldn't let go. In desperation, I furiously whip around and bite down hard on the owl's toe. The Eurasian eagle owl yells in annoyance, but her claws' reflex lets my wing go. I spiral downward to Arko Forest, losing control, feathers whipping around me, a small red stain blossoming on my white shoulder feathers.

In the shock of the event, I make no attempt to try and right myself, though I probably couldn't have anyway if I tried. I feel the first leaves of the canopy brush by, then rougher twigs, then hard branches that scrape my skin. I continue to fall to the forest floor, watching my torn feathers float up high in my wake and dance aimlessly. I'm in a trance, and do not feel the impact of the ground. I do not feel my damaged right wing pop when I fall on it, do not feel the sharp thorn in my claw, and do not notice the small owl in the canopy watch silently, huddled behind a protected spot as I drift off...

Narrator

Byhi hovers above, watching the snowy owl fall. She smiles, the snowy white feather in her beak. Another battle won with another feather trophy to add to her victories. That was the point. First to see who was the fastest, who was Byhi. Then to see if the owl would take back the trophy and deprive her of her victory. No. Byhi won.

She has to be the best. She has to prove herself, make a reputation. The feathers of every owl in Argon shows it, how she beat them all. Soon, every single owl in all of Argon will tremble at the mention of her name. Yes, that is her dream.

The Eurasian owl starts to fly back home, when she pauses. Something about that snowy owl...unnerved her. The snowy owl's beak-power, not to mention her flying skills, was pretty good. *Not as good as Byhi's,* she reminds herself*, but good.*

She continues flying home, feeling no remorse or guilt at all of the fate of the owl, or what might happen to it. *Someone must make sure that the gene pool is rid of losers.* She thought. And that is what she stuck to.

***

After a leisurely flight, Byhi sees another owl in the distance. Byhi's beak is drawn up in a smile. *Another trophy, perhaps?*

As the owl comes closer, Byhi realizes that he is much bigger than her. He is much more muscular and perhaps...more *powerful*. Byhi decides to change course, easing to the right, but the owl seems to have locked on to her. He changes his destination to a collision course. Byhi's mind races. She knows her reputation for fighting owls and winning is great, but she's never had a challenge. She always had taken on owls matching her size or smaller. She had never fought an owl that exceeded her own size, besides that scared Snowy owl. Byhi does not know whether to dive and evade contact or be brave and hope, when he realizes what a *warrior* she is, that he'll recalculate and move on. But Byhi is no fool, and she knows that the chances of this giant owl being afraid of her are just too astronomical.

As the owl is nearing true sight range for detail, she sees he's quite handsome. This Great Horned owl is quite stunning in pattern, but she also sees that his face portrays anger. *Fight or flight?* Byhi thinks. *Definitely flight! That owl is twice my size!* She dips down, heading closer to the canopy of Arko Forest. She hears the owl growling behind her, and she knows this will be one battle that she'll always remember.

Because this time...Byhi might lose.

Chapter 2: Trouble Follows

Kari

When you're faced with a choice to hide and stay alive or foolishly try and play with the Fate Owl at the risk of your life you already know the answer. At least I do. I hide. Even when a Snowy Owl comes crashing through twigs and leaves and moss I don't move a muscle. When she hits the ground and doesn't move I do the same and stay unmoving. Even when the crimson stain on her shoulder and claw start to grow I remain a statue. No one must play with the Fate Owl. And everyone knows that is the game. Whoever breaks the game's rules loses their life. Maybe that owl broke the rules.

I shift uneasily on my branch. It has nothing to do with the branch at all, because it's my favorite vantage point and I often come to perch here. The white birch bark peels nicely to reveal a softer rest. So no, it's not the branch. It's the events and the "should I or should I not" stuff swirling in my head, along with the Two Owl's voices that try to come back to me, that makes me uneasy. And when I'm uneasy trouble follows. That is for certain.

Nara

"Cici, get down," I whisper gruffly. I unfurl a wing to cover my sister, and watch as a white streak races above us. A blackish-orange streak follows. They are gone within moments.

I fold my wing back, relax my claws, and take a deep breath. We're safe. Since we're Burrowing owls, both my sister and I have feathers that match the color of the rusty-colored clay around us. We stay on the ground mostly, and if those streaks dove in our direction, we wouldn't be able to fly in time, and our burrow would be too far to run for.

"Nara, why are you so paranoid? You watch the skies constantly." Cici asks. She looks at me with those large, round eyes. Cici's black pupils grow large as she does a pleading face. I know she wants to explore, but there's danger out there. I don't spare another look at her but instead turn my vision to the skies once more.

"Because we are not alone, Cici. There are other owls. Other *dangerous* owls."

Narrator

Think streamlined...focus. Oh, please don't kill me! Byhi thinks desperately. This is the first time she felt a twinge of adrenaline close to panic, and it's very uncharacteristic of her.

Byhi dives down, twirling and turning, twisting and shifting her wings to extreme angles in order to lose her pursuing owl. The Great Horned owl will not be shaken, and he just keeps gaining, inevitable. Byhi feels the wind change. It didn't change direction; it didn't change speed, it just...changed.

The Bleian Sandstorm is coming. And if she stays in the air, she will die. Suffocated by sand and feathers torn out by the erosion. No living creature will be spared. That is definite.

Byhi smiles, regaining her cockiness and overall confidence. She will gain another trophy from this. Another owl will fall to the ground with one feather less in his coat.

The Great Horned owl increases his speed, and shrieks with ferocity. Byhi takes one last look at the clouded horizon, then closes her eyes, pulling her wings in close to her sides as she drops from the air like a stone over a cliff. As she nears the ground, the sandstorm erupts past her like a seven-ton wall, and slows her fall dramatically. She lands on a branch in Arko Forest, and quickly ducks inside a hollowed hole in the tree. The scream of the pursuing owl rings through the forest, and Byhi lets a satisfied grin slip from her beak. She spared his feathers. But it's still another trophy; this time it's a trumpet proclaiming her greatness to all other owls.

Theo

I try to psych myself up for the flight to the branch, where the dead mouse that Ma brought from this evening's hunt lies waiting for me. It's practice for my skills at flying. Of course it won't run away, so in the end I should be able to snatch dinner.

"Come on Theo," Poppy urges as he flies over to the mouse, waiting for me. Ma swoops in and joins Poppy, nestling next to him, my two parents watching their young Northern Hawk owl finally get the hang of flying.

I ruffle my feathers, take a deep breath, and plunge out into the open air. I'm gliding over to them, perfectly acing my practice test. The wind sifts through my feathers, and flows over me like I'm underwater. I'm almost to the branch, the light of the moon making the cracks in the bark glow and shift as I grow closer.

Something in the air current changes suddenly and I drop from the sky. I hear my parents' screams as I fall and hit the branches of my home tree on my way down. I see a branch shoot up in slow motion, and manage to beat my wings once, lodging my beak into the bark and finally breaking my fall. But...this isn't my home tree. It's different. I had fallen onto a different tree.

I'm lost.

I finally locate my parents' cries, their desperate shrieks echoing forlornly through Arko Forest. My beak starts to hurt from holding myself up. *I don't think this is what beaks are for,* I want to mutter. The wind whips around me, and I feel myself slip. *Owls aren't supposed to fall! They're supposed to fly!* I think, and know that I cannot ask my parents for help; if l use my beak, I'll fall.

An orange and black streak flies past me. Could it be another owl? It's gone too fast for me to be sure. Sand starts to storm by, and soon the whole forest is swirling with the remnants of a Bleian Sandstorm.

It doesn't matter if I talk now. I cannot hold on any longer.

"Bye, Ma and Poppy," I whisper, as the winds of the sandstorm rip my beak from the branch.

Cici

"Did you see that?" I ask Nara, blinking my eyes to see if I did in fact see what I thought I saw.

"What? The streaks?" Nara asks, serious as usual. She hops around, turning over rocks.

"The white streak...I-I think it was an owl." I whisper. If the white one was an owl, she was in trouble. She was being chased.

"Then we stay away from it," my sister answers, turning away and heading back to our burrow. I'm flabbergasted, though I knew my sister would do that. She usually doesn't care about anyone but herself and me. That's it!

"But after the chase I saw it fall into Arko Forest!" I protest. "We have to..." But I don't finish. The wind changes, and the temperature drops. The sun is blocked out, and a shadow falls across the ground. Nara and I know what's going on.

"Sandstorm!" Nara yells, a roaring gale suddenly erupting from thin air. We try and make it to the burrow. We really try. But the sandstorm engulfs it, and threatens to pull us in too. We would die in a tunnel that had a dead end, killed by suffocation and erosion by sand. "Go back!" Nara orders.

"Why not to Arko Forest!" I suggest. Nara spares a glance at me as we head towards the thick green underbrush of the forest. It was a glance of disapproval.

"We are not going to approach that owl!" Nara shouts, knowing me well. Her eyes shine determination, trying to protect me from every possible danger. I smile. As bad as she wanted to stay away from Arko forest, the open desert would be even more dangerous.

"Only if the Destiny Owl will have it," I whisper, more to myself than to Nara.

Kari

I pace my branch, knowing that this owl will die if I do not interfere. But I cannot! The Fate Owl is always right, surely. The Fate Owl takes care of the rule breakers. And the rule breakers get thrown out of the game of life.

But then I hear a voice, telling me a different side of the same story. It sounds like something the Destiny Owl would say. *But the Destiny Owl will reward the warriors and true of heart. The Fate Owl will not be defeated if you just stand by and let him win.*

But who is more powerful? I ask it. The Fate Owl or the Destiny Owl? Which one do I choose?

What your heart tells you, it answers simply. *What is right? Letting the Fate Owl claim avian lives or helping the Destiny Owl save them?*

A feather floats onto my branch. It's white and delicate, settling like a snow-flake. The Snowy owl down there is dying. But will I choose Destiny Owl or Fate Owl? Who will I side with?

I must not play with the Fate Owl! I must stick with my current position. Staying hidden. But the Destiny Owl always said to help those in need...

A couple Burrowing owls have gotten to her first. My choice has been prolonged.

Now I must fly down and see who the Two Owls are playing with, who is so special as to deserve both the Destiny and Fate Owls' attention.

Nara

I lead my sister through the underbrush. The sand threatens to fill my lungs and makes me cough. Small branches and thorns scrape against my wing feathers, and I hear Cici's whimpers. If this tears up my wings, I might as well be saying I put down my sword. I won't be able to protect Cici then.

We break through into a small clearing, and pause to catch our breath and shake off the sand. That is always a danger living in the Bleian Desert, the sandstorms.

A white figure is lying on the ground, just a few yards away. I turn my head, curious. Cici does the same, judging the distance. I hear her gasp. "That was the white streak," she breathes, almost sad. Cici cares about everyone. No matter whom they are or what they've done. I hardly care about anyone else except Cici and myself. You'll get the military glare if you get between me and my sister.

Cici steps closer, and I lag behind to watch her, just in case. We are finally close enough to see how bad the situation is for this Snowy owl. Her shoulder is painted a deep red, and she has a thorn lodged deep into one of her claws. On top of that she is missing a couple feathers here in there, not only from the fall but probably from some kind of battle...

"Is she alive, Nara?" Cici asks, almost pleading. I feel sorry for the owl, not for the actual Snowy owl but because my little sister had to see this.

I peer over the Snowy owl. She looks to be in bad shape. I'm about to take a closer look at how far the damage extends when I hear the soft clip of talons leaving a branch for flight. I'd know that sound anywhere.

I whip around, and see a Saw-whet owl gliding from a concealed spot. She looks cautious and uncertain. A glint of fear flits across her eyes as she lands on the ground and hops towards the fallen Snowy owl.

"She is alive," the Saw-whet owl confirms. I examine her, trying to read her strengths and weaknesses.

"How do you know?" I ask in a deep and threatening tone, baiting her into telling me what her business here is. The Saw-whet owl seems just slightly unnerved.

"I was nearby during the crash," she mutters, as if regretting it. I'm intrigued by this owl, unsure of her position and always second-guessing what to do.

Cici mutters something about the Fate Owl, and looks at both of us, pleading.

"Well, we can't let her die, can we?" she screeches, unusually desperate. It's quite an outburst, even for her.

I get to work, deciding that action is the best response. The Saw-whet owl is slightly shaken up, but still helps me lift the Snowy owl.

"We have to get her off the ground and into a tree," I sigh, and the Saw-whet owl complies. As we fly laboriously, holding the Snowy owl by our claws, the Saw-whet owl speaks.

"My name is Kari," she says.

"Nara," I grunt. I hate hauling something while I'm flying. Even though I'm an owl, I prefer huddling in my burrow. "That Burrowing owl down there is my sister Cici." Kari nods thoughtfully, but says nothing more. We both sense Cici's strong worry as she starts to follow us to monitor our progress.

We set the snowy owl down in a hollowed tree, located high on a second story. Moonlight streams in, illuminating the space to reveal that it can comfortably hold all of us at once. Cici hops onto the lip of the hollow, and turns her head sideways, studying the injured owl. She gives me a sad look that says, *I'll help*, and starts gathering leaves and benite moss to help the Snowy owl. She is probably the best one to help the owl medically, since she used to bandage up every little thing that passed by our burrow, so I leave her to work. Kari exits the hollow, and hops onto a branch, leaning over the edge. We both look over the landscape in awe.

The sandstorm had raged through here hard. The trees on the edge of the forest are covered in sand. Sometimes

I forget how vast the Bleian Desert is. Rocks are lodged in tree trunks, and thick branches litter the forest floor. It might have been a tornado for all the damage it did. Not to mention how the sand took the bark right off the trees. Just imagine what that could do to an owl.

Chapter 3: The Fallen

Theo

I wake up, everything aching. I try to get to my feet, but there's a rock ceiling. No, I'm *under* a rock. The rough limestone scrapes my feathers as I crawl out.

The forest floor is covered in a small layer of sand. The bark has been stripped off the trees. I can't imagine what would've happened if I'd stayed out here. When I fell, I...I remember catching a draft, just for a second, to stop me from spinning. I must have fallen and rolled underneath the rock. If I hadn't been shielded...just look at the trees.

I remember Ma and Poppy's cries. Maybe they made it out. I hope they didn't stay flying to try and find me. Then I will never be able to find *them*.

But do I move on or try and find them? I remember the stories of this place. I thought I was deep enough in the Arko Forest to be safe. The fringes of the Arko Forest get hit with the Bleian Sandstorms. They call that edge the Rhodes of Time. You know, like how the sands of time erode everything?

So. Get it together. I'm lost. Ma and Poppy are possibly gone forever...I'm somewhere in the Rhodes of Time. I'm unscathed from the sandstorm.

If I don't move to a safer spot I could die from another oncoming sandstorm. That might have just been the first wave.

And my options...get on the move or stay behind for Ma and Poppy?

Arne

Red blossoms in my vision as I try to make sense of where I am. Blotches of a Burrowing owl and a dark cavern are all I can decipher. My surroundings are alien to me. My shoulder hurts immensely, and thoughts quickly flash through my mind of never flying again; I shake it off, and attempt to sit up. I start to use my right claw but it feels as if it's been skewered. I screech, and try and sit up again.

I hear a muffled cry of surprise from the owl. I unfurl my good wing, and try and flap it to aid me in standing. "Wait, you shouldn't strain it. Please wait," a small voice pleads. I'll have none of it. Until I know I'm not in danger I'm not listening to anyone, whether they're on my side or not.

I screech again, and close my eyes. Everything's spinning, and it's frustrating. I hear two more birds scramble over into the cavern, and I let my efforts go into overdrive. The little Burrowing owl called backup. They seek to contain me.

I open my eyes, yellow irises dilating. Three birds are staring at me. One looks ready to pounce, one is scared, and the third looks regretful.

I squawk loudly as a show of my power. "Talk fast," I demand. One Burrowing owl looks annoyed, and wants to walk up to me and screech in my face, but what looks like her sister speaks instead.

"I'm sorry, we're just trying to help," she mutters.

"As of right now I have no reason not to plow through your pathetic line of defense and escape. What do you want from me?" I shriek. They all flinch, even the burrowing owl warrior.

"We don't want anything from you, we just wanted to help..." the small owl stutters. The warrior takes pity on her sister, and joins in.

"I'm Nara," she begins, "This is Kari, and this is my little sister Cici. We just wanted to help." Nara seems annoyed at her own self, and I can see the obvious; it was little Cici's idea, and Nara was simply going along. Little Cici beams at Nara. I can see that even Cici knows that this must be quite a stretch for the warrior owl to say she cared.

I grumble, anger and instincts subsiding. "I'm..." my voice trails off.

"What?" Kari asks, mystified. I glare at them, and then return to grumbling.

"My name is Arne," I answer, trying to gracefully fall back down. I struggle not to show the pain on my features. The three owls approach cautiously, talons scraping along the floor.

"Where did you come from?" Nara asks suspiciously, "I thought snowy owls lived in the Dilecta Arctic."

"We do," I growl, "I just got here." Nara looks unsatisfied, but I turn away, unwilling to give up anything more. Cici steps forward with wings hovering by her sides, curious.

"Well," she offers, "You can stay here until your wing is better." I turn towards her, sitting tall.

"I accept your offer," I answer, a little gentler. Cici smiles, and goes back to picking through the healing benite moss to find the right pieces. Nara slowly steps away, still watching me as she approaches the edge of the hollowed tree. Kari follows her lead, but seems hesitant, as if she's unsure of the situation to begin with. They dislike my presence. They don't trust me.

"We'll patrol," Nara says, nodding to me, from one military owl to another. I nod back, a hint of gratefulness hopefully shining through. Nara turns and jumps off the ledge, dipping down from sight, then rising on the air currents and beating her wings to soar off into the thick forest.

Kari mutters something about the Two Owls, and then follows Nara. They disappear as golden and brown streaks against the green, swirling like colors on a canvas. I sink back down and close my eyes for a moment, finally allowing myself to rest. If this is a trap, I'm dead, but what can I do about it?

Narrator

In the center where the Worte Marsh, the Dilecta Arctic, the Bleian Desert and the Arko Forest meet is a small set of cliffs. These cliffs are called Opus, and they're riddled with caverns.

However, the most desirable trait about Opus is that it has a view over all of Argon.

A bird shifts in the darkness. *Soon*, she thinks, hissing to herself, *I will have my chance. Soon I will have my Player to set the game in motion. Soon.*

The soft clipping of the Great Horned owl's talons echo in the cavern, and the small bird turns to meet him. He hobbles, weakened and sandy but still mighty compared to most owls. The Great Horned owl bows. "Your orders, Pauraque," he asks humbly. The commanding bird is impatient, unable to stay still. Then, she relaxes herself, calming at a thought.

"Survey the area, and find suitable pawns for the game," she says coolly.

"As you wish."

"How did the last chase go?"

"I believe we have a potential Player."

A cross between a laugh and a hiss escapes from the commanding bird's beak. "Bring her in," she orders, as she turns to look out over the landscape. Dilecta Arctic's draft ruffles her feathers. The sweet smells from the Arko Forest waft in, the Worte Marsh's chorus of sounds reaching the cavern. The Bleian Desert twinkles like a desert jewel. *This...this will all be mine.*

The Great Horned owl nods in respect to the bird, as five Short-eared owls come behind him, adorned in armor and trained to do nothing but follow orders. The troop of owls approach the edge and jump, flying in formation towards Arko Forest like a squad of aircrafts ready to drop some nuclear bombs.

Narrator

Byhi walks on golden sand, rising from a hollow. She ruffles her feathers, letting sand fall from them in sheets. Byhi preens them carefully, making them shine. *I should look like a queen,* she reminds herself, pausing her grooming to fly to a higher branch. She envisions a palace, with her royal feet perching on the throne and seventy servant-owls waiting on her wing and claw. *No owl should live without the pleasure of serving me,* she thinks, continuing to preen on her high perch.

A deep and powerful hoot rumbles through the forest, making her perch vibrate. Byhi nervously looks around, quickly trying to locate the hoot's owner. That call is strong and familiar, and it sends shivers of fear down her.

A band of armored owls appears from the shrouds of the canopy, swooping in together with perfect formation. The leader is a Great Horned owl...

The one that was supposed to be dead in the sandstorm.

He nods off to his right, and the five Short-eared owls peel off, adjusting their formation. His eyes burn with hatred, locked onto Byhi; his course doesn't waver, aimed straight for her. He wears a brass metal helmet and golden tips on his claws; the wind ripples his feathers as he gains speed. Byhi shrieks and tries to fly towards the sky but he knocks her down, and they both recover enough to start lashing out in flight, beaks ripping out feathers and claws raking against each other. Byhi screams, and grows frantic. She's being defeated.

This time there will be no sandstorm to save her.

Byhi shrieks once more, but the Great Horned owl gives one last blow. She falls from the air, lifeless, and a call from the Great horned owl brings three armored Great grey owls, who carry away Byhi. The Great Horned owl smiles.

"She shall not lead me into a sandstorm ever again," he growls, as he hovers to watch the Great grey owls take the Eurasian eagle owl away. He turns, and heads toward the direction he sent the rest of his band. "One part of the mission down. The Player has been secured. Now to find the pawns."

Kari

Nara and I have been sent to patrol. I don't truly patrol, but try and figure out what side I've chosen. I went along with helping Arne. Then again I didn't voluntarily contribute. So I haven't chosen, technically. I think.

Nara coasts in front of me, scanning the landscape with precision and purpose. I try and match her moves, but wander, unfocused, every time I think of her little sister. Already I can tell how different they are from each other. Cici wants to help and trust everyone and hasn't seen any real danger. Nara seems more realistic, but also doesn't usually seem to care about anything very much. She remains emotionless, eyes slowly picking out the elements beneath her. Nothing fazes her.

For a split second Nara freezes, and if it weren't for the draft she would not have stayed airborne. "Get down," she whispers hoarsely, and we immediately bank to our left and quickly land onto a branch. I come in so fast I almost fall off, but Nara catches me and breathes heavily, eyes darting across the skies. One second passes. Then two. Then a formation of dangerous-looking owls appears from nowhere, suddenly soaring in the sky. They search the ground, obviously looking for something.

I look at Nara with new eyes. She could be a fugitive. The way she watches them with fierce concentration, registering their every move. Once they pass over, she turns to me with frustration.

"What have you brought here?" Nara demands.

"What have *I?*" I shoot back, "Where have *you* come from? Are you on the run?" Nara recognizes my same conclusion and realization dawns on her.

"Arne," she growls, her anger then turning to growing fear, desperation spreading onto her features like a virus.

"No! Cici!" She takes off like a jet, flapping furiously towards the hollow. I don't know whether to follow or leave this to the Fate Owl.

"Forget the Fate Owl," I hear myself say, "Follow her." I take off from the branch, surprised at my own actions.

Apparently I've made my decision.

Cici

Nara comes screaming in, breathless. Then she sits there, catching her breath, acting confused.

"You're alright Cici?" she asks, walking towards me. I continue picking through the benite moss and putting it on Arne's wounds. I nod. "Yes...why?"

Nara refuses to return my gaze, but I instinctively know she found something on patrol. Her eyes search the ground, refusing to lift.

"I was just checking," she mutters, walking back to the ledge.

A scream pierces the chattering of Arko Forest. "Kari!" I gasp, dropping the moss and jettisoning out of the hollow. The burst of open air makes me falter, but I continue flapping my wings, soon hearing Nara's wing-beats following close behind. I look down on the trees. A small Saw-whet owl and terrified Northern hawk owl are encircled by five Short-eared owls. These Short-eared owls are equipped with shining armor and dangerous-looking weapons.

"Kari!" I screech. I dive down, gasping from the force of the air shoved down my lungs.

"Cici!" Nara warns, still high above. I ignore her. No innocent owl should die if I can help it. Especially not

Kari. She helped us with Arne; she could've left but she stayed with us. There's something about Kari that makes me instantly bond with her. Arne is a little edgy, but I would be too if I woke up with strange owls surrounding me in a strange environment.

These armored owls...they're what Nara saw on patrol. That's what she didn't want to tell me. Now Kari has to face them. She must have lagged behind too much and ran into them.

The band of armored Short-eared owls has metal-pointed talons and copper masks; their golden eyes seem washed out and without spark. I shout my most terrifying battle-cry, and dive right into one of the soldier owls. He only utters a muffled squawk of surprise before he falls. I scream at the soldiers that try and advance, and they pause in surprise, taken aback. Kari takes advantage and knocks another owl from the sky, but three are left, and they catch onto our strategy.

Theo

You will never know how terrifying it is to be in my situation. You've lost your parents, were almost killed in a sandstorm, and have been chased by a scary-looking group of owl-soldiers who want to capture you.

Their dull golden eyes show no emotion. "Come on guys, we're all owls," I mutter, as they use their talons to hold me by the scruff of the neck. I get no proper response but deep growls.

I don't know why they wanted me. They don't act as if they had been searching for anyone in particular.

As if the Destiny Owl has been watching, a beautiful Saw-whet owl flies from the blue, straight for me. I think she is meant to be my savior until she stops short in confusion. The Short-eared owls turn towards her, circling her. Before I know it, I have drawn another innocent owl into their trap.

Was she who they wanted? Was I supposed to be the bait?

A booming battle-cry erupts above me, and as I look up, a Burrowing owl barrels straight for the soldier-owls. She knocks one down, and she and the Saw-whet owl try and fend off the soldiers by screaming at each one as they come close. But the soldiers learn and soon the two owls aren't enough.

A third owl comes into battle, her fierce screech interrupting the soldier's thoughts. She tears through them like a whirlwind, a flurry of brown Burrowing-owl feathers and slashing talons. With the three working together, we are free from the Short-eared owls within a matter of minutes. They hover, recovering, the smaller Burrowing owl beaming at everyone.

I'm trembling. In shock.

"Exciting, isn't it?" the warrior owl laughs, still breathing heavily. "I like the feeling of it. The rush."

"This little owl says the 'rush' is too much," I whimper. The three owls finally focus on me, realizing that I am here. The smaller Burrowing owl smiles warmly, and motions with her wing for me to follow them.

"Come on, this way," she beckons, starting to fly back the way she came. I don't budge. These are strange owls.

As if reading my thoughts, she introduces herself. "I'm Cici," she begins, "Right there is my sister, Nara, and that Saw-whet owl over there is Kari. You'll meet Arne back at the hollow." I'm definitely unsure, and am reluctant to finally move on without Ma or Poppy, but I follow nevertheless. What else could I do?

We fly in silence. I try and hold myself together; Ma and Poppy always said that I was a funny little owl. That I could never stop making jokes. But I didn't say a word. You can't make jokes when you're depressed, otherwise they'll just turn out to be seriously depressing themselves. However, my thoughts were interrupted as Cici looks back at me with shining eyes.

"What's your name?" she asks, trying to start conversation. I try not to bring up the memory of how Ma and Poppy said that my name was special just because it was mine.

"Theo," I announce, with a little confidence for once, "I'm Theo."

Arne

When I wake up again, everyone's gone. I stand, frantically scanning the hollow. It seems as though my claw will never be the same despite the benite moss, but I can manage. My shoulder, however, was still a painfully fresh and open wound.

I limp around, but find no one. I calm down. *No reinforcement soldiers are coming to take me away...no reinforcement soldiers are coming to take me away...*

I hobble back over to my spot and wait. The Dilecta Arctic's cruelly-cold winds blast into the hollow, even though I'm located deep in the Arko Forest. I close my eyes. They remind me of home. When the ground was covered in pure-white bitter-cold and when you looked at the sky it was white with the streaks of snow. I belonged there. I had remained there until the Eurasian Eagle owl chased me from my home.

The returning owls land on the ledge, and pause to see if I'm awake or not.

"Thanks for the heads up," I mutter, opening my eyes and looking at Cici, Kari, and Nara perched on the opening, with a Northern Hawk owl nervously watching me with both fear and curiosity.

Cici looks apologetic, and Nara a little guilty. "We didn't mean to leave you..." Cici begins, but I rise, intimidating everyone as I am the largest owl in the room. I eye the young Northern Hawk owl.

"What was the situation?" I question.

"Cici went after Kari," Nara informs me, "Kari was surrounded by some soldier-like Short-eared owls." Kari looks a little embarrassed.

"I bumped into them after patrol...they had Theo with them." She says. The little Northern Hawk owl tries to smile, waving his wing shyly.

A dark, nagging feeling settles in my gut. "Were they *all* Short-eared owls?" I ask, trying to mask my growing fear. Nara looks at me curiously, as if she could sense that I was worried.

"Yes," Cici answers, unknowing. I turn away for a moment, thinking, eyes darting on the floor.

"Good," I breathe, and leave it at that.

But that feeling won't go away.

Narrator

The Great Horned owl trudges in, five battered Short-eared owls following behind him, the three Great grey owls carrying Byhi at the back of the sad parade of owls.

The commanding bird has her eyes closed, resting in the darkness, collected and in control. The Great Horned owl clears his throat, and the bird's eyes snap open. She turns to face her defeated procession of warriors.

"What have we here, Rikki?" she coos, watching as Byhi is carried before her by the talons of the Great grey owl-soldiers. They bow and step away, taking their place near the back of the party of owls. The Great Horned owl bows as well, gesturing to the motionless Byhi.

"She is your *Player*, Pauraque," Rikki answers, holding his bow. The bird looks satisfied, and smiles a little.

"Well done Rikki, phase one of the set-ups has been completed. What of the pawns?" she says, preening her feathers. Rikki seems troubled at this, scrambling for words as he keeps his head bowed.

"We have located them, Pauraque, but we shall train a few more owls and set them to the task this next round." He answers respectfully. The bird again seems contented with this news, and shuffles back to the shadows of the cavern, turning to the view of all of Argon. The arctic, the marsh, the desert, the forest...all *hers*...

"Train the owls, and loose the chase in a few days." She pauses. "What kind of owls did you run into, Rikki?" Rikki starts to relax, realizing the Pauraque was in a smoother mood, and was patient with him.

"Two burrowing owls, a Saw-whet owl, and a Northern Hawk owl were what we found. However, they flew to a hollow, and there might be other accomplices."

"Take all precautions," the bird orders, and then turns around once more to face Rikki with brown eyes. Now, Rikki was never fooled by first impressions. But this wasn't a first impression anyway. The bird's eyes were brown, but not sweet like melting chocolate. They were boiling and layered, like a witch was concocting some foul poison; the depth of her plans showed through those eyes. This bird was willing to go far for what she wanted.

"Do not lose those birds," she says. There is pity in her voice, as if she doesn't want him to fail, because his failure would mean that she would have to kill him.

Rikki gulps, an affect only *this* bird could do. "Yes, Pauraque," he answers nervously, bowing his head and leading the procession of owls out of the Pauraque's chambers. For some reason Rikki has never wanted to stay with that bird for very long. He has seen a winter wolf before, and he hadn't been fooled by its power. But this bird, this bird makes him feel weak and insignificant with a single stare of those brown eyes. Rikki shudders at the thought of her.

In the cave, the bird settles, closing her burning eyes. "Yes," she hisses to herself, "All owls shall be owned by me."

Kari

When I was with these owls, I felt right among them. Yes, all we owls were solitary predators minus the burrowing owl sisters; but I think that was the key to all of it. Cici was the key. She could make our two warriors (Nara and Arne) laugh; she could make the new young owl Theo feel at home, make *me* stop worrying or trying to decide something. Cici was the key to our current happiness.

A couple days pass, and Arne continues to grow stronger and more distant. Everyone can sense that she is disturbed since the attack. She seems partially relived that there were only Short-eared owls, but at the same time she is even more troubled.

Everyone also knows that I fret over something, and am always uncertain. Cici looks awkward every time she goes near me or Arne, and has bonded more with Theo than anything. Once he got over the initial shock he has started telling jokes. I asked him to stop...so many jokes...

"Okay, okay, here's a good one. What do you call an owl with a sore throat?" Theo asks Cici. Cici is bewildered, and shakes her head, smiling.

"An owl that doesn't give a hoot!" Theo exclaims. They both double over, laughing. "Here's another one. Someone said you sound like an owl." Cici smiles and looks at him quizzically, trying to figure it out.

"Who?" she asks. Theo smiles, nodding his head as Cici realizes she just said the punch-line. More laughs. Nara smiles at their playful nature, trying to set up her nest.

I try and throw some leaves over my head to go to sleep as the sun comes up, creeping over the trees and igniting the heavens in orange sky-flame.

"What's an owl's favorite song?" Theo asks Cici. Even Arne is listening now.

"I don't know."

"Three blind mice." He says. Arne laughs, a hearty but terrifying sound like happy thunder. "What do you get when you cross an owl with a mouse?" He pauses, as everyone over-thinks it. "A dead mouse!" he exclaims. Even I laugh, as the hole hollow is listening.

"I'm hungry," I mutter, giving up on trying to sleep. "Anyone for a bedtime snack?" Arne nods.

"I'm hungry too after Theo's jokes," Arne flashes a smile at Theo, "But I need to test out my wing anyway." Arne walks to the brink of the hollow. I catch up with her, and we both plunge into the open air, swooping sharply upwards and soon soaring high above Arko Forest. The forest looks like it's burning as the sun heaves into the sky, its rays like liquid fire. It shines and dances on the emerald-faceted leaves, like gems in an inferno. It is the most beautiful thing I've ever seen.

Arne flies awkwardly for a moment, and then straightens out, calming her wing-beats and trying to fly smoother. She seems so pure against the fiery emerald sea, and I wonder about her. She seems distant, besides her paranoia and military-like personality. What unnerved her about the attack? What was her revelation from what we told her?

Arne glances at me, then does a double-take. She sighs. "Everything's fine," she lies, sensing my thoughts, "It's just..."

"Mouse!" I exclaim, accidently interrupting Arne and losing focus. Ironic how I wanted to ask Arne about what was wrong, and when she finally starts to tell me I direct the attention away from the matter. Maybe I don't want to know. Don't want another thing to worry about, another thing to scream at me that I shouldn't have chosen to side with the Destiny Owl and save Arne.

I dip down and pluck a mouse from a pine-branch, holding it tightly in my claws. Arne spots another, and snatches it up. I start to fly back to the hollow, and Arne follows, our wings gliding on the air currents; the intense fire of the sun starts to lessen, soon *illuminating* everything more than dying it blood-red.

We land perfectly, perching on the ledge. Everyone tries to settle in, nestling under leaves or in comfortable nests. Slight snoring comes from Theo's corner, as a pile of moss rises and falls with each sound.

Arne and I finish our mice and burrow into our beds, whether it is moss or leaves or a nest of dead pine needles. I dive into a pile of leaves, not *my* kind of bed, but good enough. I drift in and out of sleep, but cannot fully rest.

The soldier-owls haunt my dreams. Their dull golden eyes, their metal masks and metal-tipped talons don't leave my thoughts. Every time I'm almost asleep the same dream replays and I'm awake again. In my dream I am flying, and they slowly turn, like zombie-owls. They screech and everything slows, where their copper masks glint maliciously and their brass-tipped talons shines, outstretched for my neck. Then everything goes black.

I give up trying to sleep. I lift my head, and see that Arne and Nara are awake as well. The midday sun creeps in, brightening the space. I squint through the harsh light (compared to the normal soft glow of the moon), and move my pile of leaves closer to the rest of the group. The presence of the two warriors calms me sufficiently, and I eventually slip into restless nightmares.

Arne

I cannot shake the feeling. It haunts me, like I should know something, like there are dots to connect. But the dots are too *far* to connect! What *should* be connected? I was attacked by an owl. I am rescued by a group of miscellaneous owls. Some soldier-owls attack the group.

Am I being tracked? Does some-bird want me dead? Is that why I was chased? I was badly damaged and perhaps was going to be dragged off to be killed by that Eurasian Eagle owl. What about these new owl-soldiers? Are they reinforcements, to find me and finish the job?

I hear Kari lift her head and move closer. I smile, and sit up enough to see everyone. Nara seems to be awake as well, eyes darting, as the wheels in her mind turn rapidly.

"Nara," I whisper, and she focuses on me. "Would you like to go for a short flight?" Nara nods gratefully, almost embarrassed. We rise from our nests, careful not to wake the other owls, and creep to the ledge, jumping out and spreading out wings. I wince as I spread mine. It hurts, but I know I should stretch it continuously.

We fly in silence for a second, just looking out at the forest in the sun's light. It's so different, and I don't think I like it. I like the concealing shadows of the night.

I study Nara, a soldier just like me. She doesn't look at me, but stares into the depths of the mighty trees, her face portraying her mixed emotions. She was thinking about her sister's safety. "You were unnerved when we told you about the Short-eared soldier-owls," she starts off. I turn away a little, thinking.

"I can't help but think I'm missing something," I confess. Nara looks at me with a slight coldness.

"Tell us the truth." She orders. She pauses, seeing my hesitation. Nara flies a little closer, trying to close the gap. A military presence replaces the coldness and she becomes inquisitive, wondering what plagues my thoughts. "Who chased you, Arne?" Nara asks. I sigh. It's inevitable.

I take a deep breath. "I lived in the Dilecta Arctic, and had no previous quarrel with any other owl. Everything was in its rightful place until she came.

"I just scored a mouse. I was on the ground, snow in-between my claws. Behind me I made out wing-beats. The snow constantly rained down, drifting on bitterly cold winds. I did not turn around yet. No owl had ever challenged me before then.

"She tackled me from behind, but I rolled so that it didn't do much besides superficial damage. I immediately took to wing, thinking I could lose her in the brewing snow-storm. But she was relentless.

"By far she's the most powerful and agile owl I have ever met, and it was a challenge to stay ahead. She was foreign to the Dilecta Arctic though, and as we cleared the arctic I saw that she was a Eurasian Eagle owl. She followed me to Arko Forest, and by then my wings were sore. I lived on the far edge of the Dilecta Arctic. It seemed so far, so far to be chased, your mind racing, your heart pumping rapidly as if it was its last beat.

"I have never flown that hard or fast, ever. She eventually caught up enough to be only a yard or so behind me. I tried to calculate, tried to make sense of it..." I get lost in the memory, and realize I'm losing speed. That's what I had done. Thought too much, let my fear take hold. That's how I almost lost my wing.

Nara stops, and joins me in a hover. She sees how my eyes dart, and my breath comes short. She seems genuinely interested, almost concerned at why it scared me so much. "...I...I lost speed. She dug her talons into my shoulder. I managed to bite her claw and she let me go by reflex, but I fell to Arko Forest. I didn't have the strength to try and right myself even if I could. Then, I guess the group found me." I try to avoid her gaze, and she herself looks like she's recalling what drove her to me.

"Cici and I saw you and that owl." She begins, "We saw you fly to Arko. Cici wanted to follow because she said she saw you fall, but I said no. That was until the sandstorm hit.

"We were too far from the burrow, and we were neighboring Arko anyway. We made it just far enough to escape the wrath of the Bleian sandstorm when we found you.

"Kari swooped down, told us she saw you fall. Cici would not leave you, and so we carried you to the hollow." Nara pauses, putting in her own thoughts instead of just telling the story. She blinks, almost confused, and furrows her brow. "I don't know why I helped. I never do stuff like that. I guess it was because Cici cared so much. She cares about every owl, you know." Nara pauses. "We should get back." She recommends, gesturing towards the hollow. I smile in agreement.

"I've had enough confession-session." I admit.

We glide back to the hollow, and walk back over to our spots. I settle down, trying to calm myself into a little rest.

The dark nagging feeling hasn't left me.

Narrator

Rikki perches on a pine branch, concealed by the canopy. His brass mask shimmers once in the light as he turns his head, peering upwards at the a couple owls above. Browns are visible, perhaps even some white.

The Dilecta Arctic is far away from here. Everyone knows that the snowies live on the far edge. It is impossible for one to be this far from home, he reminds himself, trying to get another look. An anxious Bay owl soldier starts to fly after the owls, but Rikki silences his efforts with a wave of his wing.

"Steady," he orders, "We must see where they're going." He climbs to the top of the tree, and sticks his head out of the pine needles. In a small hollow-part of a tree, on the second story, he sees a small Burrowing owl hop inside, settling into a nest. He smiles. *Perhaps there wasn't another accomplice. We can take these little owls.*

He uses his wings to direct the squad of fifteen owls. The Bay owls split into two groups, one larger backup set, and a smaller distraction party. Rikki leads the attack party, flying in soundlessly. They'll never know what hit them.

They settle beside a tree, waiting for a moment. He motions for two Bay owls to act as surveillance, and to confirm how many owls are concealed within the hollow. The two fly out noiselessly, and soon land inside the hollow. It seems as though everyone was sleeping, and the two Bay owls step inside. They fade from sight.

A minute passes, but they don't come back out.

Nara

I lay there, Cici snuggled next to me, giggling slightly as she dreams. Trusting Arne was a big deal for me. Here I was, asking how she got here, and I reveal my fears, my thoughts. *She did too,* a voice inside me says, trying to justify my actions.

A small gust of wind hits my face unexpectedly, and I anticipate a small breeze, but that's it. No other wind disturbances follow. I sit up slightly, to see two Bay owls creeping around the hollow, with copper masks and brass-tipped talons like the Short-eared owls we'd fought a few days ago. I let my eyes fall on Arne, who has sat up slightly and is watching the two owls, slightly surprised but calculating how to pounce on them. The two Bay owls turn around, and seeing Arne, jump back. She springs from her spot, and takes them down. They wiggle out of her grasp, the two working from each side to twist her bad wing; Arne stifles a screech of pain, and then hurls them into the side of the hollow with such force they are unconscious before they hit the floor.

Arne staggers back, clutching her wing, closing her eyes. It bleeds slightly, and I know it's been reinjured. I run over, inspecting it. Cici taught me a little of what she figured out, being a caring owl and all.

"You're not going to be able to fly with that," I tell her, and she sighs.

"There will be more coming. These were probably just here to size up the competition. The rest could be waiting just outside like a pack of wolves." Arne says, sitting down. Kari starts to stir, and lifts her head sleepily from the pile of leaves she had chosen. She looks at Arne, then at her damaged shoulder, then at the unconscious soldiers and back. After a few seconds she bursts from her pile of leaves, scrambling towards us.

"Wha-what happened?" she shrieks, bustling around the scene. "Fate Owl, what's going on!" Arne shushes her, hobbling over.

"Be quiet," she hisses, "The rest could be listening. I bet you we're about to be attacked." Kari looks at the Bay owl soldiers, and her eyes widen.

"They-they came back for us," she whimpers, "They really want us dead."

"Or captive," I add hopefully, though neither Arne nor I believe it. It was for the sake of calming the rest of the group.

Theo and Cici come from behind us, understanding what happened based by our exchange with Kari. "What do we do?" Cici asks, rubbing her eyes with a claw.

"I'm sitting my tail down right here," Theo answers, plopping down on the floor of the hollow. I nod to Theo.

"Cici, Kari, and I will go fight the Bay owls." I tell them, as our small band start to head towards the door. Arne steps forward, her wing hanging, slightly limp.

"I'll do what I can," she starts, and then lets an evil smile crawl across her beak, "You lure them in here and they'll be taken care of." I nod in appreciation, and take off. I hover, out in the open and a perfect target.

I look around, trying to hide the frantic edge to my movements. A brass mask gleams in the gloom of a pine tree, and I stop, tensing. The Great Horned owl growls in anger, realizing that we'd taken out his reconnaissance owls.

Seven Bay owl soldiers erupt from the shadows, led by the Great Horned owl's cry. Kari and Cici try and cover my flank, and the Bay owls close in, a tight circle strangling us like a noose. They lash out, a blur of glowing metal and feathers, and we do our best to fend them off. Cici takes a blow to the head and falters.

I screech so loudly the seven Bay owls cringe, and knock them down in a rage. They all plummet from the sky until only the Great Horned owl is left, hovering and staring at us in surprise. I'm still angry from the Bay owl clobbering my little sister, and stare the Great Horned owl down, my eyes probably looking like hot coals.

"You touched Cici," I growl. I suddenly erupt in a rage, flying closer to him. "Your owls *hit* her! Go ahead! Touch her again, and see what happens! *SEE WHAT HAPPENS!*" The Great Horned owl is slightly stunned, but gives a series of hoots, trying to calm down and hide his emotions.

Another wave of Bay owls, eight strong, reveals themselves from a concealed branch a few meters away. They give a shriek as one, meant to intimidate us. I am unwavering and unimpressed.

Kari seems nervous, and Cici intensely scared as they hurl themselves through the air, but I am an immovable boulder, designed to protect my sister at all costs. I screech as loudly as I can in return, and we clash, a flurry of yellow talons and biting beaks. A few Bay owls fall to the ground below, but we start to tire. *No!* I motivate myself, *do not give up! Cici is with you! You must not lose her!*

Half of the Bay owls are gone. We're winning, barely, but we still have the upper hand. That is, until the Great Horned owl calls in one last wave of owls.

Three Great grey owls glide towards us, flanked by two Short-eared owl sentries. For a split second the Bay owls part, and each of the Great grey owls pin us by our wings, holding us in their claws. In a matter of seconds the battle is over.

The Great Horned owl smiles as the four Bay owls and two Short-eared owls stand guard, flanking us. "Perfect pawns for the Pauraque," he muses, and motions for the

Great grey owls to follow him back to where they came from, to their base.

"No!" I yell, squirming and trying to bite the hands of the owl that was unfortunate enough to get stuck with trying to fly with me. Kari seems frozen in fear, as if she can't move. Cici is breathing shallowly, eyes darting around in fright. It is up to me.

"No!" I hear, almost an echo. A small Northern Hawk owl comes out from the hollow, screeching and looking desperate. We lock eyes. He's scared, but he wants to save us.

The four Bay owls give a sound, something like a howl, and charge him.

Theo

I am crazy. I cannot help them. What could I do? Make the soldiers die from laughter? Give them stomach aches from giggling so hard at my pathetic rescue attempt? Will *that* be my next joke?

I pace around, ignoring Arne. She seems so tortured not to help, not to be in the heat of battle. I can stand not to be in danger. Who wants to voluntarily put their neck on the line? *Apparently I do if I want to help,* a voice inside me mutters. Yeah, just waltz right in there and save them all. No biggie.

I hear screeches, and I realize Nara is probably leading them to victory. No need for my help, right?

I then turn my head to catch a series of hoots and more clashes of metal. I peek out, and see the three surrounded. Four Bay owls attack them from all sides, and now Great grey owls and Short-eared owls are swooping in. The Great greys weave in and pin the owls that once saved me, squeezing them with their talons. A Great Horned owl, obviously the leader, smiles, and says something to them. He turns, and leads them away from the hollow. *No! I cannot lose them!* I think, and in one bold move, I dive off the edge. I hear Arne cry, "Theo!" but I'm already out in the open. I yell at the soldier owls, "No!" and screech as terrifyingly as I could. Nara sees me, slightly frightened for her sister and knowing I'm scared too. But I need to get them out of there, help them escape.

I screech again, and apparently am worth chasing. The four Bay owls howl, charging me. I shriek in terror and use my wing to clobber one, kicking another in the face. I swing my other wing around to knock the wind out of a third, and I almost close my eyes, waving my talons around wildly. Two of the weaker Bay owls drop and the other two look dazed and surprised at the same time.

I grin impishly, using a final head blow to one of the owls with my wing and sending it spiraling to the earth. Only one Bay owl is left, who is narrowing his eyes and trying to hover in front of me, flexing his metal-tipped claws. I smile, something that unnerves him, and we lunge, slamming into each other. I fall back a little, knowing that this kind of fighting won't use my size to my advantage. So I fly away, making him chase me. The Great Horned owl grows impatient, and sends the two Short-eared owls. I squawk and try and fly faster, beating my wings hard. They follow me, and I falter for one second at the thought of what would happen if they caught me.

This makes me slow down; condemning me to the very thing I was dreading. I feel the cold steel of a Short-eared owls talons grip me, pinning me with her claws. She flies back to the Great Horned owl with her prize, a muttering Bay owl following behind. The Great Horned owl smiles.

"I guess I was right the first time, you did have accomplices," he says, flicking a claw in my direction.

I struggle against the Short-eared owl, but find it impossible to break free. This owl is big, and trained for holding unwilling owls like me.

With a deep hoot, the Great Horned owl once more leads the rest of the group away, and I have to make a joke.

"Watch your grammar!" I shout at him. He turns, surprised and intrigued.

"Excuse me?"

"Watch your grammar!" I repeat, "Do you know what an *educated* owl says?" The Great Horned owl is stunned, and I go ahead and say the punch line.

"*Whom!*" I hoot, imitating the Great Horned owl. It wasn't much, but I crack jokes when I'm under stress. The Great Horned owl turns back to leading the band away, unimpressed.

"Maybe I'll save you as my personal jester," he mocks, "Maybe you'll like that better than the Under-Hollows." The feathers on my neck stand on end.

"The what?" I ask.

"The Under-Hollows, where all our useless owls stay to work the rest of their lives," he repeats. I suddenly grow frantic, trying to bite the Short-eared owl. I can't get away! I'm going to be a slave for the rest of my life!

Then I remember something, actually, some-*bird*.
"Arne!" I scream. There's a pause, and the whole band of
soldier owls stop, the Great Horned owl studying me
from behind a battle-mask. "Arne!" I scream again, and
this time a piercing screech answers, something that
even the Great Horned owl proceeds to tremble at.

"The snowies…they're not supposed to be here…" he
mutters under his breath, watching the hollow nervously.
Another piercing screech strikes terror in the soldier
owls, and they grow fidgety. "It's not possible!" the Great
Horned owl shrieks.

Then Arne glides out, her yellow eyes having flames
licking inside them, like the burning sun. That owl is
angry.

Arne

Theo paces, probably debating on whether to help or
not. I feel useless at the moment. I'm the best suited for
battle and my wing is injured. Just their luck.

Those two Bay owls were trained, I know it. They took
either side of my wing and worked together to twist it. I
felt it pop. I am foolish to think it is usable yet.

But I cannot stand here! Both Theo and I know this.
What if the attacks are all my fault? What if I'm the
target their after? Cici, Kari and Nara cannot stop them
alone. If these owls are launching a second attack, this
time it will have numbers.

Theo puts on a determined face and dives over the
edge to help them. "Theo!" I hiss, but he's gone. I'm the
only one who is wimpy enough not to be in battle. Oh
Owls, why do I have to stay behind, especially right now?

I hear screeching and struggle, then finally one of Theo's jokes. I don't think they're socializing over a cup of tea, so Theo must be nervous. I bet their plan to defeat these soldier owls went terribly wrong. *'Their plan went terribly wrong.' You* think? A voice inside me mutters.

"Arne!" I hear Theo shriek. I turn my head to make sure it was him. "Arne!" he screams again, and I screech in response. I give my best screech, piercing and full of power. I ruffle my feathers, and get ready for flight. I can hear the terrified chatter of the soldiers now. They know who is coming.

I screech again, and jump off the ledge, spreading out my wings. My shoulder wants to hang limp, and I falter, about to lose control. But my anger fuels me, and I adjust my flight to manage a smooth soar over the treetops. The pain wants to take my breath away, wants me to fall from the sky like a stone, but my anger suppresses it. My right wing burns like fire.

Kari, Cici, Nara, and little Theo are all being held by owls, pinned by their wings; my rage boils, and I'm sure my eyes show it. A Great Horned owl looks at me, trying to mask his desperation and absolute fear; for a big owl like him to be scared out of his wits, I must be pretty scary day-to-day.

I hover in the midst of the panicked faces, and screech again, showing my power. *I hold your fear in my claws*, I want to say, *I shall be your worst nightmare.* I look at our little group of owls, and feel the anger once again swell inside of me.

"Let them go!" I boom. It resonates in their masks, ringing in their ears. From mindless terror I see their claws start to flex, to let my group go, then stop from the years of training they must have undergone. The Great

Horned owl hides his emotions and puffs up to defend his band of owls.

"No," he says defiantly. I screech again, drawing it out. All of them cringe, even the Great Horned owl, and I exercise my appearance of power. I continue to hover, showing off my six-foot wingspan. I can stand three feet tall, taller than any other owl I'd ever known. Even this Great Horned owl, although above average, only could've stood two and a half feet tall, hovering with only a five foot wingspan.

"Let them GO!" I boom again, forcing it. The soldier owls start to relax their claws, but the Great Horned owl growls at them.

"Hold your ground!" he shouts, and I burst into action. With a single blow I take out the Short-eared owl that was standing guard, and turn to the owls that are holding my friends. *Friends*, one side of me huffs, *you don't have friends! These are simply owls who you have spent time with during your recovery!* Another part of me shakes its head, and answers, *I care about their safety like they did mine, don't I?*

I start with Nara's Great grey owl, slamming into him and grabbing Nara from his grasp. He loses control and falls to the trees below. I release Nara slowly, and go for the owl that holds Kari. I have to free the ones that can help me first, and then we can storm the other owls and get the little ones.

I'm hit from behind. I don't make it to Kari's Great grey, and lose a few meters, trying to straighten out. The Great Horned owl looks down on me, now all-warrior and no fear. I give a short hiss and climb to the heavens, meeting him and locking into combat. His talons flash, going for my feathers. I deflect and clobber his head with a wing. He's disoriented but not knocked-out thanks to a higher-quality battle mask, and seems angrier than before. *Well* obviously, my snappy side comments. *Shut up,* I tell it, advancing.

I grab an owl's metal mask and hurl it at my opponent. As he recovers and turns toward me it hits him square on the beak, and he spins a little, like a ballet owl. I take my chance and charge forward, crashing into him again. He falls, but locks claws with mine, and we both go down. I clip the wing of the Great grey owl that was holding Cici, and then we are gone, plummeting far below. We fight with our talons, vainly flapping our wings as we spiral down like dancing partners. I hear my companions' screams above, but I block them out. Though the world spins and rolls around us, I lock eyes with his, and he locks with mine. Two warriors fighting, maybe even to the death. Neither will back down unless forsaking his honor.

But that doesn't mean I can't escape this time. I wiggle out from his grip and catch the wind, stopping my spiral. A battle to the death can wait.

I watch him fall, his eyes still locked on mine.

Cici

Arne flies toward us out of the blue, screeching so loudly all of us cringed from the volume. She tells the Great Horned owl to let us go, but despite her threats he doesn't. She frees my sister, and then tries to free Kari. But the Great Horned owl tackles her, and he requires all of her attention. Nara frees Kari, the two fighting off the Great grey owl. They dodge and weave, eventually bringing it down and then turning towards the issue of saving me and Theo.

"Nara," I whimper, as the Great grey owl growls above me. He keeps a firm grip; my wings start to hurt and my feathers dampen from sweat. I'm not sure if it was his or mine, but we both have fears, and rights to it.

"Let go of her," Nara roars, staring down the Great grey owl. Nara starts to approach the Great gray owl, absolutely infuriated; everything about my sister is tense and ready.

"Let. My. Sister. *Go.*" Nara growls slowly, her prowess very large for such a small owl, her talons twitching at every word.

Before she can pounce on the owl, Arne and the Great Horned owl stray closer, and Arne clips the Great grey owl's wing. He falters, trying not to lose balance. He over-compensates and starts to decline, keeping a firm grip on me, dropping from the skies.

Nara yells my name, and then she's diving too, yellow eyes locked on me and panicking. The Great grey owl will not let go, having his own personal meltdown. Although we owls fly every day, our worst fear is falling from the sky.

Nara manages to catch up to our speed, and bites down on the leg of the soldier-owl viciously, causing him to scream in agony. She lets go as he releases his grip, and Nara grabs my foot, hauling me up and allowing me to regain my balance. We quickly ascend in altitude to rescue Theo, where Kari is doing her best to keep the Short-eared owl in place. I flap my wings harder, my heart pounding faster. Theo is probably the most personable owl I'd ever met. I recall all the times he told jokes (even though it has only been a few days), and try and put that into every stroke. I smash into the Short-eared owl, and to my surprise it shrieks and let go of

Theo. I fly under Theo, giving a gush of wind to make him stop spiraling. We lock eyes for a moment. All of his thoughts, his fears, and his gratitude wash over me in that one moment.

The moment is broken as I hear Nara shout Arne's name, once again diving and slicing through the air. I look down; Arne and the Great Horned are locked in a spiral, falling fast, intertwined in battle. White and sooty-orange blur into each other, all stiff wings and gripping yellow feet. "Arne!" I yell, half-crying and half-pleading. I vainly dive to catch up with Nara, wanting to help so badly. Those two owls are coming dangerously close to the tops of the trees, ready to be skewered.

My heart is in my throat. *Pull up, pull up, pull up,* I scream inside, the wind stinging my face. The intense stomach-knotting feeling leaves me in a panic.

Then Arne is free, catching a draft and straightening out. The Great Horned owl still has his eyes focusing on hers. Then he disappears, past the canopy.

Nara

All of us rush over to Arne as she stares where the Great Horned owl fell. Kari follows her gaze, and Cici and Theo try not to look, who can't stand death, being little more than owlets. Arne hovers there, just staring, and I can tell what's happening. The replay of his death repeats over and over, tormenting her. That same thing happened the first time I was put into a survival situation and forced to defend myself with all necessary force. It wouldn't leave me alone.

Then she shakes herself, and starts to falter in flight. She mutters something, grunting a little as she momentarily drops a few inches.

She drops a foot now, struggling. I can see her internal fight, trying to stay conscious. Silently, I guide her downward, using her lack of strength to ease down from our height, getting ready to land. Unfortunately, she perches on a branch close to where the Great Horned owl fell. One of his feathers is caught in a web of spindly twigs at the end of the branch. It quivers in the slight breeze, and I hope Arne doesn't notice. She doesn't need to second-guess her actions.

"Owls," she gasps, breathless, "I hope you got that 'cause I'm not doing it again." Theo laughs, appreciating her attempt at a joke. It lightens the mood a little, making smiles spread on all of our faces. Our smiles die away though, as all of our eyes rest on Arne's red-soaked shoulder. She masks her pain well, and doesn't show anything besides her shortness of breath. We sit there, looking out over the forest. I see the trail of feathers where the owl fell, but no owl; my gaze finally rests on a patch of grass that seems flattened. Folded over, just in that one spot. But again, there's no owl. It's...out of place.

Interesting.

A rustle in the leaves. Theo starts to say something, probably a joke to break the silence, but I shush him. I furrow my brow, and turn around scanning the skies. My eyes take in every detail, but now everything is deathly quiet. I strain my ears and eyes. Nothing.

My mind goes into overdrive, reeling. The escape was too easy. That was just a distraction round. If we had anticipated them the first time, if we had taken out their reconnaissance, then they'd send in the Great Horned owl and his soldiers. But after we had supposedly defeated him we'd never expect another wave.

I gasp, realizing it was all a trick. To make us vulnerable, and not expect a second attempt so soon.

Whether that was their plan or they called in backup, it didn't matter. Something wasn't right. We're being watched, aimed at. But who's their target?

My eyes rest on Arne. *Are you the one they're after? Are you the reason for all of this?* The puzzle piece doesn't fit. Where's the Eurasian Eagle owl? Unless Arne lied about that detail—unlikely that she would—how did it fit together? Too many uncertainties to draw conclusions from, too many variables, possibilities, potential lies. Only one thing is relevant and worth solving: *who* are *these owls?*

Metal-tipped claws materialize from the darkness, and I barely deflect them, throwing the owner onto the ground far below. Ten other owls follow suit, most of them armored Great grey owls, with a few Short-eared mixed among them. I back up, protecting my sister, and Kari steps in front of Theo; the smaller owls of our group must be protected. Arne stands, getting a grip on herself and hiding her shallow breaths.

A particularly confident Short-eared owl steps forward. A brass mask rests on her beak, and metal covers adorn her wings. I hadn't noticed those before.

"Surrender quietly and no more harm will befall you," she eases, eyeing our group. Her expression reads *pathetic little owlets.* From behind us Arne steps forward, and the Short-eared owl's expression changes to surprise, then neutral.

"What do you want," Arne demands with a growl, her tone stone-cold and emotionless, giving away nothing.

"Pawns," the Short-eared owl answers simply. The brass masks must be a sign of leadership. The Great Horned owl had one too.

"Leave us," Arne threatens, unfurling her wings to protect the group. Her wing's enormous expanse unnerves the band of soldiers, making them shift uneasily.

"We will not leave without our prize," the Short-eared owl presses, tensing. She considers, and eyes each one of us. "My name is Celfina, and I don't know if you've heard of me but I have a reputation of getting what I have my mind set on. We will not leave without our pawns." Arne remains unwavering against her words, not even flinching under Celfina's eyes that are full of determination and fire.

"My name is Arne," Arne says simply. Celfina grows rigid, recalling.

"I think I remember that name," she begins, "I'm pretty sure I remember another snowie talking about how you took down a winter wolf. You're supposedly the top of your species." Celfina now radiates new-found respect, and her body-language asks for a challenge. Arne grows impatient.

"What do you want with them?" she screeches, increasing the volume in her voice to create the desired effect. Everyone gets the message. Arne was done with introductions.

"I want you in the Under-Hollows." Celfina states, stepping closer. Arne grows tense, angling her wings. She turns her head, examining Arne. I watch from over Arne's bad wing, doing my best to put on a warrior-like expression, watching Celfina's every move.

"Why," Arne pushes, lifting up her feet one by one and readjusting her position. Her talons clip and scrape on the rough pine-branch, as if they were steel being dragged against rough rock.

"The Pauraque demands it," Celfina answers in a rough tone, as if despising that there was another owl above her in rank. She moves in on us, trying to get past Arne. Arne screeches at the top of her lungs, a battle-cry full of brute force, anger, and rivalry. It makes everyone's blood curdle, and stops Celfina dead in her tracks.

"You will not touch them!" Arne roars, getting in Celfina's face and making her back off. Celfina nods just slightly to one of her Great grey owls and he moves in, quick as lightning. He is about to fling me away when Arne hisses and snaps, using a claw to bat him aside. It strikes his beak and slaps him, sending him back to his position, now wearier and thoroughly embarrassed. Arne lowers her center of gravity, spreading out her wings further and hissing at all the soldiers. Despite the utter blanket of fear, apparently the soldier-owls fear Celfina and the consequences of failure more than Arne. When Celfina motions for them to attack, they only hesitate slightly.

All of them pounce at once, grabbing us. Arne knocks them off the branches, rescuing us quickly. The force of her blows aren't enough to send them spinning out of control however, and they soon fly back up to their positions, striking again. One snatches Cici, and flies away just fast enough to avoid Arne's reach. Arne is unable to stretch further without risking exposing the rest of us, and seems tortured at the situation.

"This is an example of what happens if you resist," Celfina coos, and the Great grey soldier owl digs a claw into Cici's throat, preparing to go deeper.

"No!" I scream, frozen in fear and unable to leave Arne's physical fortress of safety. Celfina smiles at my efforts, and nods to the soldier owl. He presses harder.

"No!" I scream again, and I look into the Great grey soldier's eyes. He's big, bigger than all the rest. He holds Cici calmly, pressing his claws ever deeper. He stares right back at me, daring me.

"No! Stop!" Arne booms, but Celfina and the soldier owl ignore her, and Cici shrieks in fear. Arne thinks for a moment, then blurts out, "Stop! I'll go!" The Great grey owl stops pressing, and Celfina turns her head in intrigue.

"What did you say, Arne?" she asks. Arne seems almost regretful, but also responsible.

"I said I'll go with you," she repeats. Our little group is stunned, wanting to say no to Arne. But Arne continues. "I'll go without a fight. Just let the little owl go," she says softly. Celfina is slightly disappointed but also happy at Arne's defeat. The soldier owl releases Cici, and they pounce on Arne, two large Great grey owls holding her by her shoulders. Arne shrieks in pain as one grips her dislocated shoulder. Celfina gives a satisfactory smile, but orders the Great grey owls nevertheless, "Be careful of her wing." Arne looks tired, but masks her defeat and rallies her expression. She lifts her eyes to me, the spark in them gone, masked by hidden pain and loss of fire.

"Treasure what we could've lost," she half whispers, half orders. I nod, and see how she's surprised she cared about us, putting her own life on the line.

The large Great grey owl holds Arne forcefully, and looks at me one last time. His eyes are calm, but searing.

His stare says *pitiful little owls. Next time you shall be mine.* And his gaze sends shivers down my spine.

Then they lift Arne away, Celfina giving one last cold look at our little group. Her expression reads *I'll be back for you*, and then she's gone too, all of them melting into the sky's never-ending vastness. I slowly turn to the group, face slightly fallen and brow furrowed again, eyes resting on the branch below me. Theo and Cici try to look up to me, searching for some hope. Kari seems especially finished with her warrior-act, now once again slightly uncertain of everything. She seems like an owlet too, trying to draw some sign of courage or leadership from me, something to hold onto. I give them nothing.

"Come on," I finally say, "Let's go back to the hollow."

Narrator

Rikki felt like he had fallen from the sky.

This would be accurate, because he really had fallen from the sky, fighting an enormous Snowy owl. She had let go at the last moment though, and he'd slipped, not being able to stop spinning and crashing through the canopy. He'd recovered fairly quickly, and suffered hardly anything serious. He'd woken up to one of his Short-eared owls standing over him, ready to help him to his feet.

"Celfina has been sent to finish the job," the owl told him, and Rikki cursed. Of course, whenever he failed Celfina would be there to see it, to fill in his position and succeed where he had slipped. The Pauraque hopefully wouldn't notice Rikki's mistake when she would be focusing on Celfina's success. Either that or she'd be fuming because the victory would remind her that Celfina finished the job correctly and he'd failed again. Yet again.

"We should get you back to the base, sir," the Short-eared owl says, nudging the Great Horned owl to the skies. Rikki ignores him.

"Go back to *Opus*? No," he says, overriding him, "I want to see this for myself." Rikki had seen the reinforcements fly in, calm and ready to take on anything, but he'd like to see how they handled that Snowy owl. No way had Celfina been informed of its presence in the group yet. What she had been told was that Rikki had been beat by two owlets and a couple of juveniles.

He wants to see the look on her face when she sees that owl. A fully grown, abnormally huge Snowy owl that was protective of these smaller targets.

Her face turns out to be indeed priceless when the snowy owl emerges from the group. Celfina starts off with an introduction, but of course no one seems to be affected. She works for the Pauraque, and no one exists under the Pauraque's service. Celfina is just another shadow that disappears when you got close, like a mirage. In fact, Pauraque never existed, the wisps of rumors are exactly that—rumors. The Pauraque's work is known to no one. At least, it would be until it is too late. Till the game is set too far in motion to be stopped.

The Snowy owl answers to Celfina's introduction. "My name is Arne," she says, carefully considering its importance. Rikki almost falls off his concealed perch. This is *Arne*. The most fierce, renowned Snowy owl ever to soar over Argon. Everyone who has visited the Dilecta Arctic knows she took down a winter wolf once. The most dangerous part is that she cannot be blackmailed because she has no family or anyone she loves, and that she works alone. If one thing could be said about this unpredictable owl it was that she takes orders from no one.

That was, until, Celfina almost kills one of the pawns. Foolish yes, and Pauraque would be furious for the loss of a pawn, but it would make a point. She takes a small Burrowing owl and is about to slit her throat when Arne gives herself up. Astounding. Arne has obviously changed because of these owls. Then again, you can become attached to practically anyone within a few days, and Arne has never spent any time with anyone.

Celfina holds true to her word and only takes Arne with her, but I knew she'll come back. Now that this group is headless and without leadership, they will surely fall. We'll come later and pick them off, one by one. Each squad will go after a single owl from the group. Simple. Divide and conquer.

Celfina makes two Great grey owls carry Arne away, and Rikki launches himself into the air, ignoring his sore wings. The Short-eared owl soldier follows him, adjusting his tilt, wavering on the wind. They pass the canopy and break through into the miles of sky that lie before us.

"Do you wish to follow Celfina or head directly to Opus?" the soldier asks.

Rikki squints, scrutinizing Celfina. "Let's head back to Opus. I'd like to talk to the Player."

Chapter 4: Whispers in the Mist

Narrator

Byhi wakes up in a dark room with a dirt floor, a single protected torch illuminating the space. The room is as tall as three owls of her size stacked on top of each other—tall enough for Byhi to fly in. She peers up into the darkness, and realizes that the ceiling is like a cone, leading up to a single point. Byhi keeps her eyes on the top, and starts to fly.

Her wings ache tremendously, but Byhi manages to lift off the ground. The rattling of iron chains alerts her that her left foot is bound; clasped with an iron cuff. Byhi shakes the dark metal experimentally, and although it adds extra weight, she could probably still fly with it. It has a long chain, and Byhi continues to laboriously climb upwards, trying to reach the point of the coned-ceiling.

A cool breeze ruffles her feathers, heavy with night mist. Byhi is confused, but as she nears the top of the cone, she realizes it's open. It's a hole to the outside.

Byhi finally reaches the top and clambers onto the ground. No, not ground, a walkway for owls built out of worn, dampened gray wood. She rises to her feet, and slowly stands, looking around. The walkway ends in mist, the night air hanging with humidity all around her. Byhi notices a couple other holes, pitch-black expect for the gentle flicker of a torch far below. Other cone-ceilinged rooms, with imprisoned owls in them.

The Eurasian Eagle owl turns, staring into the peculiar mists. The faint whistles of the wind swirl around her and its calm yet unfocused, as if everything blends together. It is almost indescribable. The feeling the place gives her is serenity yet mystery. And at the same time, it makes Byhi's heart race with fear.

"Helloooo?" an eerie voice asks, floating on the wind. Byhi freezes in terror, but at the same time feels obligated to answer. "Helloooo?" it asks again, ending on a high note. It seems to be getting farther away.

"Yes?" Byhi calls, terrified yet her heart pounding with excitement, a strange tint of desperation edging her words like she doesn't want to lose the voice. "Helloooo?" it asks again, a final time, now almost downcast.

"I'm here!" Byhi says, but the voice has gone. The night had fallen silent, and Byhi is alone once more, standing in the mist.

Theo

Everything was terrifying but I tried to joke about it. That was until they took Arne away. Then everything became somber and serious, snapping back to reality like a whip cracking in the air, like lightning out of a blue sky.

Nara seems deeply hit from Arne's capture. I think she believes that it's her fault. When Cici was threatened, Arne felt like she needed to help because Nara would fall to pieces or hate her forever if anything happened to Cici. Nara's love for her sister created Arne's imprisonment. Or that's at least what she thinks.

Cici also looks like she feels responsible. She was the centerpiece of the disaster. *She* was the one about to be killed; a sharp talon had been pressed into *her* neck feathers.

And Kari, she is a nervous wreck. An absolute mess, though she hides it from most of us. I can see it though. She is always uncertain of everything, but now she doesn't even know what choices she has. She is utterly lost.

And then there is me. I think they expect me to make a joke about it, but I know it is the wrong time. I'm not *that* stupid.

"Come on," Nara says, "Let's go back to the hollow." She flies off the branch, heading for the hollow, not looking back to see if we follow. I turn my head sideways, looking into Cici's down-cast eyes. She smiles a little, and lifts her gaze to rest in my luminescent eyes. "Come on," I nudge gently. Kari lifts off, and then it's just Cici and me. Cici remains unresponsive.

I decide a little confession would make her smile. "You know, you're like the sibling I never had," I say, and Cici sniffles a little, wiping away a tear.

"And you're like the sibling *I* never had," then Cici pauses. "Alright, the one I really *like*. Nara's alright, but I love how you joke around." She smiles, recalling a couple of my jokes.

"Come on," I repeat, and finally she flies off the branch, both of us heading to towards the hollow. Cici half laughs half sniffles, and wipes her eye against a wing.

We gracefully land on the ledge, and step down into the hollow. Hollow...

"What do you think Celfina meant about the Under-Hollows? The Great Horned owl mentioned it too," Kari mutters nervously, perhaps directing it at Nara. Nara is silent for a moment, calculating.

"It's some kind of detainment cell or prison, maybe even a labor camp," Nara replies, "Or at least that'd be my guess." Kari nods thoughtfully, and then they both immerse themselves in their own thoughts, conspiracy theories and fears swirling together to paint awful pictures. Cici looks worried that Nara is so shaken, and I know I have to step up to the plate. This young owl needs someone to look up to.

"We should get back to bed," I suggest, but no one answers. No way could any owl sleep on events like this. "Or not," I mutter.

Cici plops down near the entrance, tears forming in her eyes. *This is all my fault,* she reads, defeated and feeling guilty. I wonder; if Nara loves her little sister so much, why doesn't she stop being selfish and helps to support her? Poor Cici is obviously blaming all of this on herself. She's barely older than an owlet! How can she be expected to fend for herself, to have no life raft thrown to her when she slips and goes overboard because of her own accusations?

I sit down beside her, and start to talk. "You know, Arne was pretty brave to stand up for you like that." Cici barely nods, not seeing how this is helping. I pause, finding the right words. "You really must have changed her." Cici looks at me with a little surprise.

"You notice how distant and crazy-uncaring Arne was?" I point out. Cici nods, admitting that Arne wasn't exactly the friendliest owl. "She gave herself up for you. She did it because you changed her." Cici seems to be a little better, now just crying for Arne's situation and not how she messed everything up.

"Arne will be back," I comfort, as she cries on my shoulder, one little owl to another, "We will *get* her back."

Arne

All of them pounce at once, grabbing my group. I knock them off the branches, rescuing them quickly. But I'm not strong enough to knock these soldiers out with one shot, and they soon fly back up to their positions, continuing their assault. One snatches Cici, and flies away just fast enough to avoid my reach. I can't overstretch or I risk overexposing the rest of the owls so they could snatch them from behind my fanned wings. I feel powerless. I cannot save them all.

"This is an example of what happens if you resist," Celfina coos, and the soldier owl digs a claw into Cici's throat, preparing to go deeper.

"No!" Nara screams, frozen in fear and unable to leave my protection. Celfina smiles at her efforts, and nods to the soldier owl. He presses harder.

"No! Stop!" I boom, but Celfina and the soldier owl ignore me, and Cici shrieks in fear. My mind races, trying to think of a way to save Cici. The strange impulse is something I'd never considered before. I had to think of anything to get her back. "Stop! I'll go!" I blurt out. The Great grey owl stops pressing, and Celfina turns her head in intrigue.

"What did you say, Arne?" she asks. I feel my old-self immediately regret what rash thing I've said, but my new sense of compassion takes over.

"I said I'll go with you," I repeat, a little more disheartened this time. My little group I'd been recovering with is stunned, wanting to say no to my decision. But I continue, trying to seal the deal with Celfina. "I'll go without a fight. Just let the little owl go." I say softly. Celfina is slightly disappointed but also

happy at my defeat. The soldier owl releases Cici, and they pounce on me, two large Great grey owls holding me by my shoulders. I shriek in pain as one grips my dislocated shoulder. It feels like it has erupted in fire, but I fight to keep my pain silent. Celfina gives a satisfactory smile, but orders the Great grey owls nevertheless, "Be careful of her wing." The last few days' events and my lack of full recovery suddenly hit me, making me exhausted in an instant. But I rally myself for goodbyes, trying to look strong for the owls I leave behind. I lift my eyes to Nara. Although it risks showing her my true state, I do it anyway. She'll see how my fire is gone, masked by hidden pain and internal battles.

"Treasure what we could've lost," I half whisper, half order. Nara nods and she sees how I myself was surprised I cared so much about them, putting my own life on the line.

Then the Great grey owls take me away. The sky ahead of me looks tainted with gray. So big and bleak. Celfina turns to me, continuing to flap her wings.

"You try anything and they all die," Celfina hisses, putting emphasis on the last word. Then she goes back to looking straight ahead, her yellow eyes cold again. The threat of her words sinks in. I misbehave and they die. Simple as that.

The scene dissolves, the slow pulse of my damaged shoulder bringing me back. I groan a little, but shake myself from the replay nevertheless. I don't want to have to relive that moment.

The bitterly cold iron bites into my right claw. It creates a phantom response, making the scar reenact the pain from the thorn that had impaled my foot. I shudder, and shake it off. I have to find out where they've taken me.

The dirt walls and floor are nothing special. But the ceiling is...is cone-shaped. Highly unlikely it's for decoration. It must have been built for a purpose.

I test the linked iron chain, and decide its long enough for me to fly up there and see its design. Another peculiar feature how the chain is long enough to allow me to have free reign.

I fly higher, taking advantage of the high ceiling. It comes to a point, and as I squint through the low lighting I realize there's a hole in the top. It leads to the outside.

What have they planned for me?

I peek my head out, leaving behind the weak light of the torch in my cell and slowly clambering onto the ground. A wooden walkway fades into the mist. I feel exposed, and turn around. Nothing but fog. But faraway whispers echo, demanding my attention.

"Helloooo?" it asks. I strain my ears but nothing follows.

My thoughts are interrupted. Wing beats from my cell alert me to my visitor. I turn towards the hole, and see an owl flying for me; she stops to grab my chain, yanking it down harshly. I screech as I'm pulled downward with immense force. As I come down I hone in on the blur and angle my fall so I land on top of the owl. As we hit the ground, my vision is shaken into focus. Celfina's eyes burn with anger, staring into mine with disgust. I catch my breath, holding her gaze with just as much hatred.

Celfina squirms a little, and I slowly step off her, never letting my glare waver. Celfina stands slowly, and to my satisfaction the fall must have weakened her slightly, but Celfina hides her ache and is now to her feet, holding my stare.

"We need to break you," she says, her words solid and dangerous, "So you can be usable material. Otherwise the Pauraque will throw you out."

"What do you want with me, what am I to *you*, if you have such rank here," I quickly growl back. It would be normal for an owl to flinch at my tone, but Celfina must have seen my kind before, because if she flinched she did not physically show it.

"Apparently you are of importance to the Pauraque," Celfina says, with a little too much cheer, "But who ever said you were anything to *me*?" She turns to leave, then remembers something.

"Oh, and prepare yourself for your first set of training." Celfina adds. Then she opens a metal-braced wooden door, and disappears, leaving me to collect myself.

Though I will let no one see it, I am worried. What if they *can* break me? What are they doing to Nara, Kari, and Theo or...or Cici? There's nothing stopping them from going back and snatching the rest of them. That's what I would do if I was in their position. Make an unsaid promise of protection and then turn around and break it.

I sit down and cover my head with a wing. Why am I falling apart? I find this new sense of compassion annoying, hindering my chance of escaping from here. If I fight back my group is in danger. This compassion opens the door to being broken in like a horse for these power-hungry cheats.

Okay...I can do a couple things. One, I could let them believe I'm broken in and work from the inside. Two, I could resist and possibly get my group hurt. Or three...I could say that they're on their own, my group, and focus on surviving.

I gradually lift my wing off my head and prepare to face my next challenge. I look up at the Two Owl's sky for guidance, and then realize...I *don't* have to face it.

I quickly fly up to the top and clamber out onto the ground. I try and walk farther but my chain pulls taut, and I strain against it. I remember every challenge I'd faced in the arctic, every winter wolf I'd faced, every single peril I'd overcome, and push against these chains, driving the memories into the metal bonds. I hear them start to succumb to my efforts, so close to yielding. But then I feel my shoulder start to stretch again, and I stop, panting.

Escaping is a mental trap, Ceflina's voice echoes in my mind, telling me in words what her body language read after I tackled her; *it is a distraction from facing that you're stuck. You'll never get out.*

We'll see, I want to challenge her, *we'll see who will yield first. And we'll see who will rule: the captor or the* captured?

The tables will *be turned. Count on it.*

Rhi

The growls of my masters seem to wreak disappointment as I fight to focus over the layers of noise. The clanks of metal sound as the servant owls' talons and beaks toil over the raw material, willing to mold it into our master's dreams of battle armor and weapons of soldiers. The very things that create war and drag more owls into this sinkhole of dictatorship.

I keep my head down and carry on the work that resembles an assembly-line of production. I falter as I polish a battle mask. It's brass. This will go onto a higher ranking owl, an owl that will give orders to his soldiers to storm someone's home. Like they did mine. When the owlet's parents have gone out hunting for a moment, to snatch her out of her nest before they come back. Then turn her against other owls, making weapons. So cruel to make the victims of destruction forge the tools of more utter-devastation.

One of the master owls comes from behind and slaps my shoulder as a warning. "Quicken your pace," he growls, and the other owlets next me whimper slightly, eyes wide and feet shaking.

"Keep working," I comfort them, giving a little edge to my voice so that they obey but just soft enough to not make me seem like another master.

"Rhi," an owl yells, and my heart skips a beat.

"Yes?" I answer, hoping the tremble in my voice wasn't heard.

"Missed one," a master owl laughs, tossing me a battle mask that had a single smudge near one of the eye holes. It was probably his own claw that had smudged the piece of metal, but I'd never actually say that, and I reprimand myself for thinking such rebellious thoughts. I catch the mask in midair expertly, one footed. A few of the masters stop, staring at me. I give a glance and continue to my work, eager to be in the spotlight no longer.

More muttering commences behind me, but I do my best to reel my mind back into what my claws are doing currently. I polish the masks and toss them into the wooden crate, moving on to the next one, then the next. Like I wasn't even thinking.

No one *is* thinking anymore. After your first week or two your thoughts of escaping or evading harsh treatment are shattered. In one way it's just like roaming free. *Adapt or die.*

***

My claws and beak are sore by the time my shift is done. Two emotionless soldiers escort me back to my room. I walk stiffly, and they basically pull me along; I'm so tired I barely hear the metal clank of the door as I settle down into my cell.

As I start to nestle in, I look up at the cone-shaped ceiling. "Ah well," I sigh, and fly up out of my cell, staring into the mists. I prepare to whisper into the night, to ask my eerie hellos, when I stop for a moment, wondering if any owl gained anything from this. I shrug it off.

Maybe one more time. Give some owl hope. Maybe some-owl will answer. That'll give me some hope to go on. Maybe.

Cici

Everything inside of me had fallen apart, until Theo glued me together, piece by piece, joke by joke. Nara had dealt with it by planning, trying to paste together all the information of what Celfina and the Great Horned owl had said. I appreciated it, but she failed to realize how much I had needed her.

After a day with Theo, I have become my normal bright self. We hunt mice and laugh as we fly, finally heading back to the hollow after a wonderful morning filled with glee. But my smile dies down when Nara calls me into one of the corners of the hollow, tracing things into a piece of soft bark with a talon.

Theo eyes the plans and notes, and smiles. "Prison break? *Sweet*," he guesses, turning his head to the side. I allow myself to giggle a little, and Nara takes the time to give a lopsided smile.

"It's a lot more complicated, and we don't have all the facts." My sister explains. "Kari's had a revelation; she's the one who pieced most of it together." Kari almost blushes, and seems eager to turn the attention away from her actions.

Nara gets her reaction, and quickly moves on. "The Under-Hollows...the Great Horned owl said it was where the Player and the pawns spend the rest of their lives, toiling," Nara's eyes dart around, the puzzle virtually fitting together as a horrible picture comes into view, "It sounds like a prison, or maybe more of a slave compound." Kari now steps in, eyeing the plans.

"Both of the lead owls mentioned pawns and players...and the Pauraque. I believe we can infer that the Pauraque is their leader, and whoever it is has a plan set in motion. Why else would the terms 'pawns' or 'Players' be used unless in a real-life chess game?" All of us nod in agreement. Theo steps toward Nara, and lets his mind's gears turn a little.

"What's our lead on Arne's location? Where do we start?" he asks. Kari falters, again undecided. I stare in horror at them, those older owls still so naive.

"What does it take to get you to care about another owl?" I ask, my tone rising. "Nara, my own sister, who else do you care about? Do you care about *me*?" Nara seems hurt by this.

"I love you more than anything else," she protests, but I make my point.

"Exactly! But you don't care about any-owl besides me. If you care so much about me, you'd see how I want to help these owls. This could be it, to save whatever owls have gone to the Under-Hollows! Not just rescuing Arne, but preventing other owls from being captured! Do you know how much that means to me?" My eyes start to sting, and I let myself lose control, letting it all out. "If you love me, then you'll help me save owls!" Nara grows angry.

"I've made sacrifices! Every day I go out to forage for you, keeping you in my thoughts, fueling my every step, my every breath. But in order to protect you, I cannot let you go out putting faith into every bird that passes by! You have to learn that not everyone is good!" Nara's eyes fall, as if some phantom pain is dredged up by a memory. She starts to choke up a little. "Some owls...evil owls would pay anything to get their claws on you. They want free labor, avian lives to do their work for them. I couldn't live with myself if they got you." I'm suddenly hit with a wave of regret for what I said. Memories of Nara coming home with bloody wings and feet, scratches from sharp talons decorating her body.

"Sometimes you'd come home...and you'd say you just ran into a really thorny tumbleweed..." I realize, tears rolling down my cheeks.

Nara lifts up her right wing and reveals a nasty scar right under the shoulder. "They'll claim your wings. They don't care." Nara's gaze falls. "Now you know."

"But that's why we have to save Arne!" I scream. Theo hesitates, thinking, then hovers at my side.

"She's right," he says. "We cannot allow it to happen." He lowers his voice, looking Nara in the eyes. "Do it for your sister."

Narrator

"Come on," a particularly pushy Short-eared owl barks at Byhi, standing at the open door. Byhi turns toward her, and snorts.

"*Now*," the Short-eared owl growls, grabbing Byhi with firm claws.

***

Byhi is shoved onto the cold floor, ears twitching as a small bird in the darkness chuckles in amusement.

"Looks good, Celfina," she coos, "But is this the true Player?" The Short-eared owl that earlier had been pushing around Byhi searches the floor, determination shadowing self-doubt.

"Yes, Pauraque," the Short-eared owl named Celfina confirms. The bird chuckles again, and small, toxic-brown eyes focus on Byhi.

"Show me your worth," she orders. There's a pause, and the bird clarifies. "What great achievements have you done?" Byhi dawns her sly smile, suddenly calm and in control, as if again expecting another victory.

"I am the best owl in all of Argon," she proclaims. The bird chuckles.

"Go on. What proves this?"

"I am the fastest, the strongest, and the smartest." Byhi opens a wing, revealing dozens of feathers woven into her own. "My trophies," she explains. Feathers from every kind of owl line her inner wing. Including a Snowy owl's.

"Impressive," the bird admits, "But you are missing one." The Great Horned owls feather is absent.

"For the trophy of the Great Horned owl," Byhi continues, "I was given a trumpet of my glory during a sandstorm." Celfina's eyes widen for a moment, her comrade's stories making sense.

"They were my screams as you led me to a potentially brutal death," a large owl booms angrily, stepping from the shrouds of blackness that hang around the corners of the cavern.

Byhi turns, and sees the very Great Horned owl that had chased her, the one that should've been dead. The Great Horned owl comes closer, talons clicking on the floor. He positions one of his talons under her neck.

"You wanted me dead," he says, "And the feeling is mutual."

"Rikki," the bird orders, more entertained than angry. The Great Horned owl backs off, taking his place beside the small bird.

"Do you want everyone to know you *are* the best?" the bird in the darkness asks, in a silky and tempting voice. Byhi's ears prick up. Of course she does. She *knows* she's the best.

"Yes," Byhi answers, like a puppy that is salivating over a bacon treat. The bird smiles, though no one sees it through the veil of gloom.

"Tyranny is such a privilege," the bird coos, "A luxury, really. Do you have what it takes to become a tyrant above all owls? To become, *Lady* Byhi?"

Arne

I lay low, listening to the orders of Celfina. Two Great grey owl soldiers stand beside her, as if they're simply to be symbols of her power and ranking.

"You all have potential," Celfina purrs, "But all of you might not make it back to your cells. After training, only about half of you will remain in the program."

She flies down and lands loudly in front of me. I keep my gaze on the ground. "No matter who favors you, no matter whatever chance you think you might have, they stand invalid here. None of you will make it out unchanged." I lift my eyes now, the sun's flames licking inside of my irises.

"I'd like to see you try," I challenge, keeping my gaze steadfast.

"That could be arranged," Celfina says through gritted teeth. It's never good to have a leader intimidated by a simple prisoner in front of all the other captured owls. Or at least it isn't good for the leader.

A small barn owl in the crowd watches me, examining my body language. She starts to unfurl her wings a little, as if she was shielding the rest of the captured owls from me.

Celfina slowly backs off, and flies back up to her post. She perches on a carved branch, once again showing off a regal prowess. "All of you will work for the Pauraque now. Your work will be known to no one, and if you are deemed worthy for missions, any glimpse of you must be dismissed as a trick of the light. Once you are activated you *do not exist.*" I start to tune out, and soon Celfina has flown down to me once more, daring me.

"Let's begin with training," she hisses.

***

"Test one," Celfina announces, "Your mindset." Two white barn owls from the back of the crowd head towards Celfina, landing without a sound on the ledge. They turn to face us, and their eyes aren't glazed over like the rest of the soldiers. They're burning bright, devious and without restraint.

"We are the Twin Wings," the one on the left shouts.

"I am Ruole," the one on the right declares.

"And I am Pyre," the one on the left shouts again.

"We will see who is weak and who is strong," they say in unison, their green eyes almost glowing. The Twin Wings search the crowd of captured owls, as if they were looking beyond.

"You!" they boom at a young Eastern screech owl, and the rusty-orange owl looks around, then nervously flies to the ledge. Pyre beckons to him, and he takes his place beside her.

"You!" they shout again, and a couple Short-eared owls fly up. Pyre again beckons to them.

"You!" they snarl, pointing at several owls. The small group flies up, and Ruole gestures next to her. They shuffle beside Ruole, casting uneasy glances at the Twin Wings.

"You!" they boom, and a small owlet quivers at their pointing talons. Nevertheless, the scared owlet flies up to the Twin Wings, and Pyre takes her.

"You!" they boom, pointing at me and the Barn owl that had watched me earlier. The Barn owl seems reluctant to leave. Then she considers it, and flies wearily towards the Twin Wings.

"You!" they repeat, again pointing their yellow claws in my direction. I stay still, and everyone around me is searching for who the Twin Wings had chosen.

"Arne!" the Twin Wings yell, and I look around me, then take flight. I beat my wings, silent yet powerful. I gracefully land on the rocky shelf; the gray stone and rubble feels icy beneath my feet.

"Come," Pyre beckons, showing me the way with a wing. I take my place beside the Barn owl.

"Are you really the one who took on a winter wolf?" the Barn owl whispers. I nod, but don't take my eyes off the floor. The Barn owl doesn't say anything else. She seems like she's planning; anticipating my next move.

Celfina eyes the Twin Wings. The two snowy-white Barn owls see their cue and their emerald eyes gleam as they glance at each other.

"These must go," Ruole proclaims, gesturing to the owls she had picked.

"And these must stay," Pyre declares, waving to the group I'm in. The barn owl beside me seems very surprised, as if she were muttering, *what did they see in me?*

Celfina seems slightly surprised as well, but hides it expertly. She eyes the Barn owl with blazing yellow eyes, and then turns back to the rest of the crowd. "You heard the Twin Wings! The ones that must stay will proceed ahead, and the ones that must go will be transferred to the Under-Hollows." No owl moves. "*Go!*" Celfina booms, and the gathering of owls disperses hurriedly, heading in different directions.

"You," Celfina says, inspecting us with caution. The Short-eared owls, the Eastern screech owl, Barn owl, owlet and I watch her carefully, with anticipation. "You seven will come with me."

Kari

The Fate Owl can be cruel.

Just when Cici was starting to change Arne, and make her a better owl, Arne is captured. Cici falls apart, and Nara focuses on avoiding the soldier owls. Nara needs to be formulating a plan to save Arne instead. Cici saved Arne; she was the one who brought her into the group. She won't give up now.

"Kari," Nara asks, looking at me for help. Theo and Cici are putting the pressure on her to rescue Arne. Of course it's illogical, but Cici overrides any realistic rules of trickery, deception, or evil's general existence, and presses us into saving every owl we happen to come by.

I sigh. I can't be uncertain now. "They're right," I admit, "We need to get Arne back. She saved our lives."

"And we saved hers," Nara snaps, "Now we're even."

"You know it doesn't work that way..." I protest, but Nara quickly cuts me off.

"Why doesn't it? We saved her, so she saved us from being brought into an issue concerning her past actions. We're done with this matter." Nara orders. But my mind's gears rapidly turn as I remember.

"No," I say slowly, "Celfina didn't even know Arne's name, remember? How could Arne have brought these owls upon us? They were looking for pawns. Any owls, really." Nara silently curses, and almost stamps her foot.

"The matter is decided," Cici forces, "We will save Arne, with Nara's consent or no." Nara snorts, but doesn't say anything.

"What we need is a lead, a point in the right direction." Cici prompts. We look at each other, but our faces are blank.

Theo searches the floor, apparently catching on to something. "We'll start at the Rhodes of Time."

I immediately catch on. "We're bound to find something there," I agree, "It seems as though that Great Horned owl still had some sand in his feathers."

"Then he must have been caught in the sandstorm," Nara concludes, "That means he came from beyond Arko Forest. That's a start."

Do you like death? A voice in my head asks, *because you might just meet your fate. Sandstorms can reach the Rhodes of Time. Just imagine.*

Or you could save a life, another voice reminds me, *you could be an avian hero to all owls. But fame shouldn't be your motivation. Look at Cici. Do it for* her.

Owls, I've chosen Destiny once again. Sometimes I miss the shadows and staying out of this dangerous game.

Chapter 5: Seeds of Hope

Rhi

I cannot believe I was chosen. I am no soldier. The only thing I want to do is protect all the other owls that ended up in this place, not bring in more. I'm a protector, not a fighter.

Arne, she's a fighter. She'll endanger all of us. When Celfina and Rikki get angered it never goes well for the owls on the bottom of the totem pole. That would be us, the ones on whom they take out all their frustration. Arne's stirring up the hornet's nest. She'll make them mad and then ruin everything for us.

Celfina turns, and with a great leap she is gliding through the air. The Short-eared owls follow, the scared owlet trailing behind them, and then the Eastern screech owl falls into line, as Arne and I launch into the air to take last place. The Twin Wings supervise behind us, ending the procession; their emerald eyes glow stark against their pure-white feathers.

Celfina leads us up, twisting and turning to avoid beams of gray rock. After a few stumbles the owls in front of us get it; Arne clips one of the beams and twirls upward, loosing balance for a moment. She winces, if only for a second, then returns to dodging, maintaining an intense focus. I can see a slight gasp escape her beak, and I can see her almost sweating in her effort to stay airborne.

Does Arne have a damaged wing? Would this great owl be hurt, and still in recovery? It could be dangerous for her around here; if Arne resists they'll know where to hit to get some reaction.

Celfina continues to lead us up in a steep incline, and we soon break into open sky. She lands on a gray wooden platform; the worn wood looking like it wants to creak under her weight.

"Let's divide up this group," Celfina states with an edge to her voice. "Who has the want to be a soldier of the Pauraque? Who wants to serve the most *superior* and *powerful* bird of all of Argon?" The three Short-eared owls screech loudly in response, raising their wings high as Celfina smiles in approval.

"What about you?" Celfina asks the Eastern screech owl. He nervously looks at the ground, eyes darting, uncertainty lining his features. Celfina frowns slightly, and walks over to him. She lifts his head up with a claw. "Only the strongest, most talented owls serve the Pauraque. You must have no doubts in your mind as to where your loyalties or your future is." The Eastern screech owl doesn't seem sold, but even more withdrawn now.

"If you truly want to be the best, what can you do for us? What will you give the Pauraque? Consistent agility? Ferocity in strength, or boldness in attack? What makes you better than all the other owls down there, who would do anything to get out of the Under-Hollows?" Celfina lets her claw fall gently, and the rusty-orange owl shakes a little, trying to decide.

"I-I can find out anything." He stutters, finally looking up at Celfina.

"Do go on," she approves.

"If there's something to know, I'll find out about it. I can persuade any owl, and can fit into tight spaces, not to mention that I can navigate out easily as well." Celfina seems pleased, but moves onto Arne.

"What about you?" she prods. Arne chuckles in a deep tone, threatening and full of mockery.

"I believe you know my position in this matter," Arne answers darkly. Celfina narrows her eyes to yellow slits.

"What a surprise, the great Arne resists. She obviously is not the best, is she?" Hoots from the rest of the owls ring agreement. Celfina straightens. "However, the Pauraque has ordered that we keep her here for as long as possible. She has good potential, and that must be enough for now." She moves on from Arne and onto me. This is a perfect example of how Arne's actions will make it worse for us. Celfina's going to go hard on me because she's angry with Arne.

"What proves your worth here," she growls. I stay silent. Celfina lowers her head, staring into my eyes passionately. She growls again, and surprisingly just passes me by to the owlet. The poor thing's chest is heaving, shallow breaths taken many times a second. "Why are you here? What can *you* do?" Celfina asks. The owlet whimpers, trying to keep her head down. Her terrified eyes make her purpose clear: she didn't want to be chosen, and doesn't like this scary owl at all.

"Leave her alone," I whisper. Celfina turns on me.

"What did you say?" she hisses, getting into my face. I close my eyes for a moment and gulp dryly.

"She doesn't want to be here, she's just an owlet." I repeat. Celfina's eyes burn brightly.

"*Now* you speak," she muses. "We'll use that weakness as training." She grabs the owlet by the neck, white talons pressing into her feathers.

Arne

At first it had all been a skirmish. Then Celfina grabbed the owlet by the neck, and I saw Cici's capture all over again. I hear echoes of my name being screamed as my group was captured, and this was no different to me.

I screech once, short in length but piercingly sharp, and lunge at Celfina, impacting her hard and making her release the owlet. The owlet flops down and scrambles to hide behind me as Celfina falls back, gasping. I growl once, deep in my throat, and lift my wings so I shield the Barn owl and the owlet. Just like I did for Nara, Theo, and Kari.

I slip into that memory, and I growl deeply. Right now that Barn owl and the owlet are my group, and no one will touch them.

Celfina slowly gets back up, angrier than ever. She hops over and screeches at the top of her lungs. I join her, and we aim it at the sky; everyone can hear mine boom above hers, still stronger in volume. After drawing it out, we stop, slightly breathless.

Celfina's eyes widen as she draws the connection of my actions. Her eyes narrow and she almost laughs. "What did they do for *you*," she snorts, dismissive of my old group's actions. I give a cold stare, arctic fire showing through my yellow eyes.

"They saved my life," I snarl. I feel the Barn owl shifting behind me; she can sense the history between Celfina and me.

Two large Great grey owls try to attack from behind. I whip around and deflect them, letting them fall from the platform like acorns from a tree in autumn. My wing explodes in pain, but I hide it expertly, and adrenaline helps suppress it. I will not let it hinder me in my mission to protect these owls. Celfina screeches for a moment and five more owls materialize around me, and the Barn owl raises her wings to protect the owlet, eyes watching them with weariness and a warrior's sense. *No wonder she was chosen, she'll do anything to protect owlets like these. They could corrupt that*, I think.

I launch myself into the sky with a booming hoot, and in one fell swoop I plow through the soldiers, the circle around us disintegrating into fear. Most of them are plucked from the air and fall to the gray platform of wood with a creaking thump. Celfina starts to chortle, the sound growing in volume and pitch. She shakes her head, pleased with herself. I lower myself down slowly from a hover, my shoulder again starting to slowly burn.

"You're right as always," Celfina admits, glancing at the Twin Wings. I growl deep in my throat. We've given away our potential. We've shown what we do in battle. What's scarier is that Twin Wings knew us and what we could do before Celfina even set up the test.

"The owlet sees what is going on and can follow silent orders," Celfina points out, "And these two, they're protectors. We'll break them though." She looks at all of us, and then glances at the rising sun.

"Get to your cells; we'll deal with you in the morning." Celfina turns to go, then stops, and pauses for thought. She faces us again, and a cruel grin creeps onto her face, starting from her beak and reaching her eyes.

"No, I want to say something." Celfina steps toward me and stares into my eyes, her gleaming yellow irises emanating pleasure in a single evil thought.

"I will make you into predators, into soulless machines that will do nothing but my bidding. Your minds will fall beyond reach and I shall make you my sword, *using* you to bring other owls to the same fate." Celfina laughs at the thought, giddy with glee.

I feel a freezing sensation blossom from my chest, and it grips me hard. It's fear; I'm afraid of turning into something like that. I fight it back and stare Celfina in the eye, letting the heat of my anger burn through the seizing fear.

"Believe what you want. I'm not going down without a fight."

Theo

The forest is eerily quiet, hung with the scent of the fallen. Sand from the Bleian Desert layers every leaf and nook of tree-bark like dust. The echoes of past owl's final screams seems to linger, forever hanging on that last note.

Ma and Poppy could've been one of them.

"What are you looking for?" Cici asks, trying to keep her voice light and unfocused on the problem at hand. My mourning is interrupted and it brings me back to the moment. I search the ground, visualizing the pattern I'm looking for.

I spot it; a Great Horned owl's feather flutters in a slight wisp of wind, weighed down under a pile of twinkling gold sand on its base. I dive down, and Nara follows my gaze, her eyes widening as she realizes what

I've been looking for. She lands beside me, watching me examine the feather. Like dogs catching a scent on the wind we both look towards our right and past the Rhodes of Time.

Nara nods to me and we both take flight, weaving through the forest. Confused, Kari and Cici follow us, wearily matching our movements. I think Kari gets the general idea, but doesn't know where we are going.

The desert sun falls onto our wings as the heat from the shifting sands below creates an instant oven from all sides. The blistering wind bakes me alive, but I just squint and search for another feather.

Nara finds it first, and dives down close to confirm it. "We're hot on the trail," she yells.

"You can say that again, I'm going to be burnt to a crisp by the time we make it to Arne!"

"Payback," Nara breathes, ignoring my complaints and rising on the thermal currents to glide beside me, "This will be what I've been waiting for."

"Exactly *what* are we doing?" Kari asks, anxiously scanning the wavering horizon.

"We're following that Great Horned owl's trail of feathers," I explain, "I knew he'd follow Celfina back to their base. Since he was caught in the sandstorm, he must be losing some feathers. I should know." Cici looks at me with concern, and I realize my mistake. They don't know that I had been in that sandstorm. I quickly move on to my point, "Anyway they should lead us to where Arne is located. We'll get her back." I finish. Cici looks at me curiously but with worry, eventually dropping the matter and giving me a chance to tell her what happened.

But I don't, instead looking straight ahead. I don't want to dredge up the memory of my parent's horrified faces, and their cries of grief and desperation, searching, trying to find their little owlet. They never found me because the sandstorm hit.

With a mental scream I let reality pull me back in, and I crash back into the situation. I have to search for the feathers, follow the trail. I miss so much as a single feather and Arne could die. That's a pretty heavy weight on my shoulders.

Narrator

Rikki walks around Byhi, who is standing before a grungy mirror with a purple silken cape. A golden clip holds it onto her shoulders, and a silver battle-mask shines and shifts with the flickering of the torch. Her eyes blaze like the torch, taking in her own daring aura.

"Will this suit your needs?" Rikki asks. Byhi smiles subtly, and nods once.

"This is sufficient," she replies, already practicing her standard answers as she has now become the supreme Tyrant of all owls. Pauraque has arranged this so that she is merely a puppet on strings, but Byhi doesn't know it. She is reveling in her own greatness, falling in love with herself.

She turns to Rikki, the cape twirling slightly at the change in wind. "When will my appearance be?" Byhi asks, her voice lower and in more control ~~then~~ than when she had faced the Pauraque.

"The next full moon," Rikki answers. Byhi looks back in the mirror.

"And when will that be?"

Rikki smiles. "Once the sun sets."

Arne

The freezing iron bite of the shackles once again adorns my feet. I slowly spin in a circle, evaluating every single line in the walls. My room seems to be hollowed out from a tree that climbed onto some kind of cave, but it's lined with dirt. The lone torch grows and shrinks rapidly, casting shadows on the wall. I run over to the door, banging against it. Locked. Even though it's made of wood it's reinforced with metal. Thick, unshakable metal.

There's only one way out: up. I climb altitude, bursting out of my cell and into the open air. I land on the wooden platform, the auburn sun creeping out and starting to evaporate some lingering fog. I walk forward, gaining speed, but my chain pulls taut. I look back, shaking the chain. I growl and press against it, creating massive amounts of tension. "Cici!" I yell into the darkness, straining against the iron. "Theo!" I shout again. I cry out in pain and anger, feeling the metal dig into my leg, and I push ever harder, testing its limits. I close my eyes, grimacing. *Never give up, don't give up now. Remember them. Remember Cici.*

The chain creaks, and gives way. The sickening sound of metal being ripped apart suddenly explodes into the silent morning, and I tumble, momentarily losing control. My vision goes black for a second.

I slowly come back into focus, feeling as though I'd flown beyond the sky and back, blood pounding in my ears. I groan, and sit up, glancing at a blurry-red claw. I shift my gaze to the rising sun. I'm so close to freedom. I could just waltz right out of here.

What's holding me back?

Beside me is another hole. I peer down, and realize that I'm looking at the Barn owl that had been chosen by Pyre earlier. She's squatting down, crying into her wings. I roll over and fall into her chamber, unfolding my wings to catch myself at the last moment. The Barn owl looks up at me with surprise.

"You...but...Arne...they..."

"No time," I grunt, and take hold of her iron bonds. I wedge my slim claws onto each side, trying to pull apart the metal cuff. The Barn owl looks in disbelief from the cuffs to me and back again. Her beak gapes as she hears the whine of the metal, cracks and squeaks coming from the restraints. My face contorts in pain as I continue forcing my will against the strength of the metal. In a sudden eruption the Barn owl's free, shards of metal flying in all directions. I'm thrown to the far wall, groaning. My vision swirls, and I hear the slam of the door as it's opened furiously.

"Rhi!" Celfina shrieks, full to the brim with absolute rage.

Rhi

Arne had come for me. She had escaped, and come back for me.

My amazement is short lived as Celfina bursts into the room. No wonder; we'd made quite a racket in here.

"Rhi!" Celfina shrieks, her eyes blazing with rage. I run to Arne, not looking back.

"Arne!" I yell. Arne grunts and nods, launching herself upward and clearing the roof. I follow, flapping feverishly to try and escape Celfina's wrath.

I feel the wind hit my face, and my fears float away. I grew comfortable too soon. An irate Celfina grabs my leg, her steely grip just challenging me to be foolish enough to struggle against it. I gasp as I immediately lose speed upwards and start to fall down, down-down-down, back to a world of constant fear and hard labor.

Arne screeches, enraged with Celfina's actions, wrapping her claws around my wings and yanking me up. Celfina's grip suddenly slips away, and I'm free. Arne carries me high up into the air, trying to put distance between us and that horrible place; she slowly releases me, letting me fly on my own.

After some wobbling I straighten out, gliding smoothly on the winds. I look up at Arne, curious about her. This owl was more complicated than I thought. "Why did you come back for me?" I ask. Arne wavers for a moment, and flaps again to stabilize. She keeps going, silent and deep in thought.

"You reminded me of someone I knew," she says strongly yet gently. With unspoken power she urges me to drop the matter, but I will not.

"Who? Who could change the *mighty* Arne?" I bait her, curious to see who has given Arne a sense of what's right.

Arne loses her focus. "A single, small burrowing owl," she answers, "Maybe her sister too, and the Saw-whet owl who had stepped up from the shadows. I guess the jokes from our Northern Hawk owl didn't hurt either." I'm intrigued, but Arne won't say anything more.

But after a few minutes, Arne falters. She grunts, and straightens out. "Is everything alright?" I ask, troubled that Arne faltered in mid-flight when there was no wind gusts.

"I'm pretty sure we've lost them, and I think I need to land," She groans, and we slowly slip from the blue sky, gliding to the trees below. Arne lands clumsily on an oak branch, breathing laboriously; I examine her, searching for something wrong. Then my eyes rest on a fading red stain on her right shoulder.

"Oh Owls," I whisper. Arne looks at me, and follows my gaze, looking at her own shoulder. She shrugs, trying to catch her breath.

"Just sore," she says, dismissing her condition, "Haven't had time to let it rest."

"What did you do to it?" I gasp.

"I was attacked," Arne clarifies, "Some owl dug her claws into my shoulder. I fell and dislocated it. I was found by some owls, and had about three days of recovery. The soldiers came and I had to do battle. Haven't let it heal since." Arne pauses. "I still haven't gotten your name."

"Rhi," I tell her, "My name is Rhi." Arne lets her head rest on the tree trunk, almost smiling.

"Nice name," she comments.

"My mom and dad thought so," I say, trailing off. Arne studies me, and I take it as a request to hear my story. I sigh, squeezing my eyes shut as I recall the memory.

"Food was abundant, and my little brother was growing fast. Mom and Dad were so proud of us." I falter, taking a deep breath.

"They...they came during the day. All I can remember...all I can remember was the coppery shine of talons and flashes of metal. They didn't care about my family. They just wanted me. Apparently I was at the right age to be a good worker for their organization.

"Ever since, I've been working in the Under-Hollows with the rest of the hundreds of captured owls who have shared my sentence. We polish masks, do whatever the masters want, and sometimes gather for recruitment. I never thought I'd be picked. They thought differently." Arne thinks for a moment, her gaze downcast.

"You developed a warrior's instinct, just on the good side," Arne tells me. "You want to protect those other owls. You're a natural-born warrior, and they could corrupt that protective nature into a mindless soldier. They want to prune you like a tree, making you grow into something twisted." I look down, letting the meaning of her words sink in.

"Do you think they could do that? Really?" I whimper. Arne sighs.

"We don't have to think about it anymore. We've escaped, right?"

I pause at her words. "I can't believe they got you in the first place."

"They didn't." Arne answers, "I gave myself up." I was about to ask why when I saw that she again didn't want to talk about it. I return to her last statement, about how we've escaped and we're home free. I *wish*.

"They'll be after us though," I protest, "If I know Celfina she won't let any owl escape for long under her watch." Arne's eyes lose focus, as if reliving a memory.

"Who were your authorities there?" she asks. I wait for a moment, running through recall and flipping through virtual faces.

"Pauraque was the highest, but we never saw her. Celfina and Rikki were the only others." Arne shakes her head, still remembering something.

"There was one other," she breathes. Her eyes widen, and I could have sworn it was with fear. "It was her!" Her eyes dart around. "They wanted me from the beginning. Either that or they recruited her just as they did with me."

"What are you talking about?" I ask. Arne finally looks up.

"We have to tell the others," she says, then does a double-take at my confused face. "That group of owls that saved me? We have to tell them."

"Tell them what?" I persist, but Arne's already stretching her wings.

"When I was attacked by that owl," she explains, wincing as she rotates her shoulder, "I managed to see that she was a Eurasian Eagle owl. When I was saving you from Celfina, a twinkle in the darkness caught my eye. There, behind Celfina, was that same owl. She was watching me with hatred, wearing a purple cape held with a gold pin. Celfina fell onto her and they both went down. That's how we gained a lead on them."

"So we're going to try and find your group?" I ask, trying to clarify.

"Yes," Arne answers, springing off the branch and into the sky. She grunts, and falters, but then straightens out again, eyes focused on the rising sun.

"Shouldn't we rest first?" I inquire, hopefully scoring a night's rest.

"No," Arne answers firmly, "We'll lose the lead and then they'll be on top of us." I yawn, shaking my head to wake up.

"Alright," I sigh, giving up, "But you might lose me about three in the afternoon."

Nara

The feather trail continues, keeping us soaring over golden sands. We have to be getting close. Theo had a stroke of brilliance with this plan, but now the heat is almost sucking the water from my body. Because Cici and I are Burrowing owls, we usually spend time down in our cool burrows, not riding the inside of a heat tunnel. Trust me; you'll never want to fly in the desert.

Something looms in the distance. "Theo, are you seeing what I'm seeing, or is it another mirage?"

Theo squints as the shape gets taller as we grow closer. "I'm seeing it alright. We're approaching Opus."

"Wait," Kari says in disbelief, coming to the head of the group to fly beside me, "You mean the cliffs? We're at the center of Argon?"

"The very ones," Theo comments. "Perfect hideout. This is where they took Arne, I'm sure of it." Cici flies next to Theo, gazing beyond and trying to see inside the maze of caverns in Opus.

"She's there, somewhere." She breathes, almost sad. The Opus is looming now, and off in the distance I see Arko Forest on my left. The Worte Marsh begins somewhere off to my right; straight ahead, right after the Opus, would be the Dilecta Arctic. The Opus is like the center in a pinwheel of environments. Argon really is a wonder. Four extreme climates, bordering each other without catastrophic consequences. Amazing.

A few owls appear on the horizon, seemingly coming from a fissure in the cliffs. Cici gasps happily, but my soldier's sense pounds in my head, making my adrenaline rise dramatically.

"It's a trap!" I shout, and turn around quickly. I grab Cici and Theo by one of their wings to turn them, and Kari follows, now taking the rear of the parade. I beat my wings furiously. I'm losing my touch. I was so stupid! Of course there would be guards, and from Arne's reaction they'd know we were close and that we'd come to rescue her. "I was a fool!" I yell, straining my abilities to try and get away while we could. But my short wings won't cut it. Really, all our wings were short. Theo and Cici were barely more than owlets, and Kari was short anyway like me. We're doomed because of my mistake.

Chapter 6: Mistakes

Arne

I stop dead in my tracks. "Oh Owls...!" I curse, turning around and heading back to Opus. Rhi looks at me with intrigue and worry.

"What is it? Could you keep me in on the loop of breakthroughs here?" she pleads. I almost laugh if the severity of my mistake wouldn't have been so dire.

"If I know Cici she would've persuaded the group to come back and rescue me," I explain, "And this whole time we've been heading the wrong direction. We need to stop them from heading back to Opus. I'm sure they're almost there." I beat my wings faster and faster, determination to save them fueling me. I grit my teeth against the pain of my shoulder and decide that from now on I'm going to ignore it. It's just been getting in the way.

Within minutes I spot a group of owls heading back from the Opus. Two owlets fly beside two other owls that are more mature. "Nara!" I call to one of the owls. Nara's shining yellow eyes focus on me, and she smiles gratefully. It's always good to have another owl that's got your back.

"Arne!" I hear Cici squeal, flying harder to try and catch up with me. Now I can see them, Kari looking more warlike than ever, Theo looking determined and radiating leadership. He gives a lopsided grin at the sight of me.

"Who are they?" Rhi whispers to me. I laugh once, something I thought I'd never do. Rhi looks surprised at my outburst as well, but smiles anyway.

"These owls are the group that saved me." I answer. "Well, not Theo. We sort of saved *him*." Cici doesn't slow down, and crashes hard into my chest.

"Oof!" I grunt, laughing. Cici snuggles up to me, closing her eyes and wrapping her tiny wings around me.

"I'm glad you're okay," she says.

"We're not quite out of it yet," I inform her gently, gesturing towards the thirty owls locked onto us like a targeting system. Nara, Kari and Theo hover around me, looking at Rhi.

"This is Rhi," I introduce, "She's an owl that was going to be turned into a soldier. I couldn't let that happen."

"Soldier sense, eh?" Nara asks. Rhi shakes her head.

"Not quite sure what they saw in me," she admits. I tell them the truth.

"Protector's instinct," I say, "She protected an owlet during recruitment. They thought they could use that." I glance again at the approaching company. They're coming in hot, and don't seem to be slowing.

I can make out the details, and I recognize who's leading the assault. All of a sudden I can't catch my breath, my shoulder burns like fire and my claw is throbbing. I falter in the air for a second, staring into those cool, psychotic eyes. It's the owl. It's the owl that attacked me, and almost broke my wing. She damaged my shoulder. She's the only creature in Argon who had gotten the best of me.

"Arne?" Nara asks, rushing over to support me. I ignore her, staring at the Eurasian Eagle owl. Nara follows my gaze and sees the owl, the memory of my story telling her how I ended up on the forest floor of Arko Forest clicking in.

"No," she breathes. The Eurasian Eagle owl screams a battle cry, and I see Rikki and Celfina on either side of her wings.

I see Celfina say something to the Eurasian Eagle owl. She's too far away for me to hear the words but I could make out what she said by looking at her posture. *Byhi, the battle is yours.*

"Byhi!" I shout to her. Byhi loses balance for a moment, and I continue. "I know your hunger for power! Give up now and escape with your life!" Byhi snorts, again, something I couldn't hear but could see.

"You are surrounded!" Byhi shouts above the wind. I smile evilly, realizing I have Byhi right where I want her.

"That is where you are wrong! Those petty forces cannot protect you from my revenge!" Byhi almost drops from the sky. I can read her expression. *Are you a ghost?*

"I am here to defeat you once and for all!" I melodramatically howl the lines, slowly and loudly, charging into the battlements. Nara sees my plan and screeches, prompting the rest of the group to do the same. Cici hesitates, but puts on a brave face and screams fiercely.

Byhi recovers, and screeches, diving for me. We collide, talons entwined just like when I fought Rikki. "How are you still *alive*?" Byhi growls, trying to throw me off of her.

"I told you," I say, "I don't die." Byhi screams and throws me down, sending me spiraling. My course leans toward the Worte Marsh and I laboriously spread out my wings, catching the wind and letting myself shoot back up like a rocket. I turn to face Byhi once more, focusing on her eyes. They were a peacock of emotions. Fear, worry, rage, and over-confidence. Not a great combination when you're facing one of the most powerful owls in all of Argon.

Her silver mask shines iridescently. She is obviously still affected by my bluffs, and I'm pleased. That was my goal. That phase was simplicity itself: play mind games. Now comes the harder part. Fight her off long enough to take on Rikki and Celfina if I can. My group doesn't have enough owls to take those two on top of the soldiers. There are just too many.

I grunt and lunge at Byhi, smashing into her and momentarily catching her off balance. I shift my momentum and fall into a Short-eared owl. The owl turns around, screeching in surprise, and I curse silently. It's a regular soldier, not Celfina. I look around, scanning the battle, and spot her brass battle-mask.

I change my course, rising on the air currents towards Arko Forest and Celfina when I'm tackled by a huge owl. I gasp in surprise, and turn to face my attacker.

"*Rikki*," I growl, and then we're locked in combat once more, talons slashing and beaks tearing. I use my wing to clobber Rikki's head, making him unsteady. The brass hurts my wing but I don't care. I don't care what hurts. What can I do about it?

Rikki recovers more quickly than I had estimated. He hits me in the face, making my cheek burn. I growl deep in my throat and give a fear-inspiring screech, raising my wings high and angling myself so I fall into him. He flies up, meeting me in the middle, and we collide with such force that any owl watching would wince.

We're suddenly losing altitude, again falling from the sky. With one foot we hang onto one another, and with the other we try and scratch, parrying attacks and searching for openings or weaknesses. We're interlocked, two great warrior owls fighting to the death. Neither will let go. There's no escape this time.

A new adversary's screech enters the fray. I glance up, and manage a glimpse of Celfina, a psychotic grin plastered onto her beak like a happy killer. Soon she slams into us, our little death-trio creating a rotating ball. With the added weight we fall faster, the spears of Arko Forest rushing up to greet us. Rikki and Celfina stiffen, waiting for impact. They don't care if they die as long as I die with them.

My eyes widen as this revelation hits me. If they go down I get dragged down with them. There's no duel to the death if they are willing to die. I have to escape.

Celfina and Rikki smile like vampires as they see I finally realize their mission. "The great Arne shall finally fall," Celfina laughs. Now I see that it isn't military tactics. It's suicide.

I struggle against their grip. The swampy ground littered with unseen quicksand traps would just love for us to crash into it. I cannot let that happen. Their talons dig into my feet and I cry out. My scarred foot where the thorn went in is throbbing, aching. I fight with everything I have, but the two combined is just enough to be my final match.

"Nara!" I scream, but she's preoccupied. Even little Cici's fighting valiantly. Kari's swooping through the soldiers, taking mouthfuls of feathers and drawing them away. There's only one owl that could help me now.

"Theo!" I cry. He turns, and his eyes widen with fear as he sees me spiraling. "Theo!" I cry again, as the swamp oaks are merely a few seconds away. No...I'm too late. No one can help me now.

Theo

I think of jokes to say in order to deal with stress, and 101 jokes are popping up in my head as the battle rages around me. Even Cici was fighting, screaming her head off and taking down owls. I am hovering, doing nothing. Technically it isn't my fault, I am in shock. I can never do what they do. I play around, and even orchestrating Arne's rescue is a huge stretch for me. I cannot do this.

"Nara!" I hear a faint plead. There's a pause, and then I hear my name.

"Theo!" someone cries desperately. I look down, and see three owls locked together, a spinning ball of feathers. One of them was white. Arne! She's being pulled down by those two other owl-commanders.

"Theo!" she cries. For once Arne needs help, and I'm her only hope. She sees the fear in my eyes and her gaze softens to one of acceptance. She's going to die.

"No!" I yell, letting myself drop from the sky. I dive after Arne, but the foliage was about to take her. I can't let her die. I'd live forever knowing that I was too scared and wimpy to try and help her. All the other true warriors are at work and have no wings to spare.

I clear the foliage, and I'm almost to them. I quickly adjust myself to be more streamlined, and as the owls rotate I slip in between two of their wings. I'm inside the circle.

It's Celfina and that Great Horned owl. I see the knot of claws on-top of each other, and bite down hard on them. The two top ones must have been Celfina and that other owl, because they cry out and struggle against my grip. I let them go and the Great Horned owl falls from the group.

"Rikki!" Celfina screams. Her eyes burn with flame but I manage to push her off Arne. We spin off from the group, watching Celfina land somewhere in the shadows.

"Thank you," Arne says, right before we hit a swamp oak. Those are words I'd never thought I'd hear from her, and it is something strangely comforting.

"You owe me," I reply softly, and then my claws slip from hers.

Rhi

I want to feel frantic, but I can't. I'm strangely calm and at home here, using cold talons to fell owls as I continue my path. I've failed. I really am a soldier, I just didn't know it. Just another cold-blooded killer.

"Hello, traitor," a voice growls behind me. I whip around, and see Byhi, the owl that Arne was so worried about. She wears a silken purple cape and a golden pin, and her silver mask glitters in the sunlight.

"The name is Rhi," I answer smoothly. I don't even know myself. I'm standing in the face of danger, calm, cool, and collected.

"So confident, are we?" Byhi snorts. I want to yell at her, *yes! But this is not me! Don't mind a word I say!* But it didn't quite make it to my beak. Byhi narrows her eyes, searching me. "What did Arne see in you?" she mutters. "Ah well, if I can't have you as a soldier on my lines then no one can." I want to ask her the same thing. *What did you see in me? I should never have been chosen to be a soldier!*

Byhi screeches and lunges for me, talons outstretched. I dodge and rake her underside with my claws. Byhi shrieks in surprise and once she's cleared my range of attack she turns, the fury at my actions blazing in her eyes.

She screeches again, and I squawk a battle cry, and we clash, a flurry of feathers. In her rage she's clumsy and not particularly careful, leaving many openings. I hit where I can, trying to eventually cripple her with the jabs and strikes. Byhi starts to lose her breath, but shows her talent when she pauses for a moment, recomposing and just sticking to parrying my moves. Metal clangs and the cries of pain from Arne's group shout for my attention, and I long to turn and help them. But the best way I can help them is by defeating Byhi.

I catch that last thought. *Defeating Byhi?* How in the Owl's Skies am I going to do that? *I'm capable;* a voice deep within me says, something I'd ignored since I was first captured, *If I can defeat Byhi then I can go help Arne with Rikki and Celfina. My old masters...it's time for payback.*

I dive towards Byhi, yelling and slashing my talons. *I must end this quickly. How can I win? What advantages do I have against her?* We bite and scratch, hissing all the way. *What are her weaknesses?* Her silver mask flashes in the sunlight, as if intentionally trying to draw my attention. *Yes, she appears to love power. But how can that help? I need an advantage now, in* battle! On reaction to Byhi's slash I dodge and punch her in her stomach, forcing the air right out of her lungs. Byhi loses a couple feet, and seems dazed.

My old strategy shall be my new one. I continue with my defensive attacks, jabbing and eventually making Byhi breathe hard, struggling to hold her balance. I hear a name being called far away, but I have to ignore it. I can't lose focus now.

More shrieks echo to my left, but the sound fades away, the background of the ongoing battle blurring and leaving me altogether. All that remains are Byhi and me, fighting, slashing, swinging and stabbing. Now even Byhi is forced into slow motion, and she makes a fatal mistake. She overextends a talon-attack, and leaves me a clear path through her defenses. I curl my claws into a fist and curve it under her chest, pushing through to her chin and knocking her off balance. With the final blow everything returns to normal, the sights and sounds of combat rushing back. The leader of the battle falls, Byhi's feathers rippling with the wind.

Most of the soldiers pause, doing double-takes, and Arne's group huddles together, watching them. The enemy owls stare at me, both in disbelief and forming fear. I lift my head to the sky and screech loudly in triumph and victory, letting all my horrible memories as a slave rip out of my lungs. I finally let the retching sound die away, and the owls scatter, a couple diving to the forest below to search for Byhi.

Cici

I've never done anything this violent before. I justify my actions by picturing all the owlets they could've captured, screaming like a mad-owl at every soldier I fight. Our band of owls seems impressed with my valor and bravery, and I swell with pride, fighting harder.

An intense screech breaks all trains of thought. I turn, and realize everyone had been watching her. Rhi lets her head fall from the scream, looking at the soldiers with the burning adrenaline of success in her eyes. They scatter, abandoning the battle.

I quickly look at everyone. Rhi is obviously alright, albeit she has quite a few slashes through her feathers. Nothing unfixable there. Kari's okay too; she's exhausted and has a single scratch near her eye, but she gives the gesture that her wounds aren't important. I spot Nara, and suppress a gasp. A large gash covers one of her legs, like someone tried to cut her leg off. She wobbles in the air, dizzy from loss of blood, and Kari goes over to support her. I spin in circles, trying to look for the rest of our group.

"Where's Arne? And Theo?" I ask. I get no reply. My medic's sense screams inside my head, alarm bells ringing, sharp and headache-creating. "No," I breathe, as I spot a single white feather caught in the leaves of a branch below me. I dive down from the sky, tears stinging my eyes. I see a crumpled white figure at the base of a swamp oak, but no Northern Hawk owl.

"No-no-no-no-no-no-no...no, no Theo! *Theo!*" I scream. I fly erratically, like a hummingbird on caffeine. "Theo!" I scream. My cries echo in vain, the forlorn sounds just bouncing back. No replies.

I hear Arne slowly rise to her feet, and her face is unreadable. Regret and guilt maybe, but a lot of sadness and inner anger. I turn back to the marsh. "Theo!" I scream again, but I know that he's not going to answer.

Why Theo? He was the only one who could put me back together. He was the best companion an owl could ever ask for. And he's dead. The owl that always joked, always made fun and kept up the group's spirits, was dead.

Arne

The impact from the tree left me dazed and slightly confused. I felt my shoulder pop out of place again, but I didn't care. Something was nagging at me.

I flex my talons. They're empty. What happened? Where's Theo?

I open my eyes and try to sit up. Pain and ache, not just physical, hits me like a freight truck. No. The impact. I remember his claws slipping from mine. But where *is* he?

I look around. I'm resting on the edge of an island, shadows shifting from the canopy, humid air clinging to me like a second skin. Marshy waters surround me.

No...could he have fallen in? When he slipped through my grip, could he have spiraled and fallen into the marsh's waters? But he couldn't be dead. He couldn't.

"Theo!" I hear Cici scream. "Theo!" she yells again. Her voice is full of pain and longing, desperation and unwillingness to give up on him. *"Theo!"* she screams one last time, before she starts to cry. I slowly manage to sit up this time, the scene around me momentarily blurring together like paint strokes.

Cici looks back at me, silently asking me to say that Theo isn't dead. For once I feel tears sting my own eyes. I want to shake my head, but my face gives it away. Cici turns her back to me, continuing to scream Theo's name.

I shouldn't have called for help. Maybe if I tried harder, I could've saved myself. Then maybe I wouldn't have brought Theo to his death. I could've fought harder...

And your wing would've been beyond repair, a voice says inside me. *I don't care!* I reply, *I don't care about my* stupid wing anymore! Theo's dead *because of me!* Then it hits me. Theo's dead because of *me.*

The wing-beats of two birds descend towards us, and I turn my head to get a better look. Kari supports Nara a little, and then Rhi descends. Rhi seems satisfied with herself, but her expression turns to worry as she sees Cici's face.

"What happened?" Rhi asks. This was the wrong question to ask, obviously, and Nara flinched slightly. By seeing our state, Nara had pieced together what probably happened, and it was not the right time to ask Cici or me about it.

Neither Cici nor I directly address Rhi's question. "Theo!" Cici screams again, and it's answer enough.

All the things I could've done better, where I could've tried harder, fly past in my mind. I could've held onto him harder...I could've defeated Rikki and Celfina on my own...I could've I could've I could've...

Screeches sound above. The soldiers must have regrouped. Rhi looks around, worry etched into her features. I stare through the canopy, setting aside my grief.

"Byhi seems like the type that doesn't give up," I mutter. Rhi shakes her head, flying towards me. A slight pride gleams in her eye.

"Byhi's down," she declares, "I put her down myself." I do a double-take at Rhi. That small owl took down Byhi? She was a challenge even for me. The Twin Wings guessed right; that owl has something special in her.

"Someone needs to draw them out," Cici says, trying to pull herself together. Nara tests her wings, but Kari puts her down. Nara should rest somewhere.

We shouldn't place the burden on Rhi, she's been there her whole life. She just got out; she shouldn't have to go back in.

"I'll go," my treacherous beaks orders, "I'll go back and draw them out." What am I thinking? If I get caught I'll lose my mind; I'm not strong enough to resist training, and I certainly am afraid of becoming a mindless killer.

"You're in no condition!" Nara protests, Kari nodding along. I forget their pleas, a single memory blinding any logical thoughts.

You owe me...you owe me...you owe me...

I certainly do, Theo. And I'll protect Cici for you. No matter if it is with my last breath.

The wind rushes up to my face, and I concentrate on that and not the state of my wing. As I break through the tops of the marsh oaks, I see ten Great grey owls waiting for me. They screech and aim for me, like heat missiles locked on a target.

I screech in response and slash my claws, taking out two Great grey owls. But there are so many, and I'm in bad shape. They swarm, overwhelming me. I scream and slash, to make it convincing. Despite my efforts they eventually have me, two especially large Great greys pinning my wings and hovering with me in their claws.

The Eastern screech owl I had seen that was chosen stands before me, a bronze mask glittering on his face and a purple robe with a golden pin fluttering in the breeze. He inspects me, a tiny hint of doubt showing in his eyes.

"Arne, wasn't it?" He asks. I humbly nod my head. He mutters something under his breath, and sighs. "I'm Intyl. Or at least, that is what the Twin Wings named me." He pauses. "I'm sorry it has to be this way, but I request you do not struggle. The Pauraque has ordered me to bring you back to Opus." He starts to turn, but stops, quickly facing me as he remembers something.

"...during the battle, the soldiers told me there were more. You were not alone." He hovers closer, searching me for answers. "Where are your little friends?" This time, I allow a flicker of my grief to show.

"Dead," I spit, looking away. Intyl nods thoughtfully.

"As it should be. It would be worse for you if Pauraque had someone she could use to get to you." Intyl seems genuinely sorry, but willing to please the Pauraque.

"Why did you fall so easily?" I ask, trying not to push it.

Intyl pauses. Though he has his back to me, he turns his head slightly so I can hear his answer. "We do what we have to in order to survive."

Cici

"I'll go," Arne volunteers, "I'll go and draw them out." Nara shakes her head.

"You're in no condition!" Nara protests, Kari nodding behind her. Arne takes one look at us and takes off, flapping hard to break the canopy.

That glance...what was she telling me? Something was off.

I hear battle screeches from the soldiers. I dry my tears and fly up to a branch to watch the battle, peeking from behind swamp-oak leaves.

Arne screeches in reply, hacking away at the Great grey owls. They surround her, and she seems to grow weak. I hold my breath. Break free Arne, break free. Use your voice, at least.

Despite my state of shock from Theo's...*disappearance*...I long to jump from my hiding spot and help Arne. But that wasn't the point. She had to draw them away from us.

They pin her wings, easily overcoming her. Arne is subdued, defeated and screeching in vain. But something about her is wrong. Something isn't right.

An Eastern screech owl appears from the battlements. He seems almost sorry for Arne, and says his name is Intyl.

"...during the battle, the soldiers told me there were more. You were not alone." He hovers closer, searching Arne. "Where are your little friends?" Arne looks like she's recalling what happened to Theo, and turns away.

"Dead," she answers.

"As it should be. It would be worse for you if Pauraque had someone she could use to get to you." Intyl seems genuinely sorry, but willing to please the Pauraque.

"Why did you fall so easily?" Arne asks, an undertone of disgust in her words.

Intyl pauses. Though he has his back to her, he turns his head slightly so that Arne can hear his answer. I read his beak. *We do what we have to in order to survive.*

Then they take Arne away, and I slide down a branch, saddened. I know what was wrong with Arne.

She knew she was going to be captured. She went willingly. If she had been trying she would've been able to defeat them, even in her current state. She had given herself up.

Maybe it was for Theo. I know she saw him go. Maybe she did it for him.

I fly back down to the group; all of them seem a little anxious. "They took her," I report. Nara's eyes widen.

"Their regroup was *that* strong?" Nara asks nervously. I shake my head sadly.

"She gave herself up," I clarify. Kari's gaze falls to the ground, as if she were realizing Arne's reasons.

"I thought she might," Kari confesses, "It's hard to draw all the soldiers away if you're running. Then the diversion's obvious. But if they capture you, if you make it convincing...maybe they'll be satisfied." Kari pauses. "What went on up there?"

"Some Eastern screech owl was there. He had a bronze mask and a robe like Byhi's. Must have been second in command. He took Arne away, but he was a little apologetic. He asked where we were and Arne said we were dead; when Arne asked why he had fallen so easily he said that he had to do anything to survive."

"Wait!" Rhi says, her eyes slightly unfocused as she searches her memory, "Was the Eastern screech owl a rusty-orange color?"

"Yes, you know him?" I inquire. Rhi nods, solemn.

"Sometimes all of the captured owls are called to gather for recruitment. There are two white barn owls called the Twin Wings, and they choose who will become soldiers and who should forever work in the Under-Hollows. The rest who aren't chosen just go back to work. They're sort of undecided. I was that for a little while, I was one of the undecided owls, but when Arne came I was picked by Pyre.

"Pyre always chooses the ones to become soldiers. Ruole picks the ones who are weak and will never be anything but laborers. Pyre picked me, Arne, a small owlet, a few short-eared owls, and that Eastern screech owl.

"When they were sizing up Pyre's picks, he finally said that he could find out anything for them. They named him Intyl."

"I get it," Kari mutters, more to herself than to the rest of us, "*Pyre* chooses the ones who can handle *Power*. *Ruole rules* out all the weak ones. And when the Eastern screech owl gave up and told them he could get information, they named him *Intyl*. Sounds like *Intel*, right?"

Rhi continues her story. "He must have been promoted or something. He led this final wave." She shakes her head, furrowing her brow. "But...his mask was bronze, right? And Byhi's was silver? Then who's is gold? I remember Celfina and Rikki's were brass. That means they weren't even one of the top generals." Rhi pauses. "I wonder where they went. Anyway...who's got the gold mask then?"

"Can you remember any other authoritative figures?" I ask urgently.

"Yes..." Rhi replies, "The big figure everyone talked about was the Pauraque. The Pauraque might be the head of this operation."

"Intyl mentioned something about the Pauraque using the ones Arne cared about to get to her," I agree. Rhi's nods thoughtfully.

"This Pauraque bird is pretty secretive though, no one outside the Opus knows she *exists*." Rhi whispers.

"Makes sense," Nara comments. Something rustles in the leaves nearby. All of us snap our heads towards the sound all at once.

"Time to get going," Nara orders.

Narrator

Byhi's eyes flutter open, and she sits upright, gasping loudly. "It's alright Byhi," two voices instruct in unison. Their voices are calm and collective. Byhi turns, and stares into two matching sets of glowing emerald eyes.

"We are the Twin Wings," they say.

"I've heard of you," Byhi mutters. The Twin Wings nod respectively.

"The honorable Pauraque has..." Pyre starts.

"...asked us to relay a message." Ruole finishes.

"*You have failed me. Rise to the occasion or perish. Secure your place among owls. Let no one stand in your way. Next time there will be no second chances.* That is the Pauraque's wishes." The Twin Wings say, their voices layering over each other's, creating an eerie affect.

Byhi nods gratefully. She knew she had failed big time. Beaten by a small, traitorous barn owl. No, she was weakened first. By that irritating Snowy owl. "What happened to that snowy owl, Arne?"

The Twin Wings smile. "Recaptured. She thought it was safe, and came up from the marsh. Intyl caught her."

Byhi flinches. She can't let Intyl take her job. "Good. I'd like to have a word with her."

Arne

I shudder. The iron shackles are cold, and now there is one on each of my feet. They make me chilled, and tonight the winds from the Dilecta Arctic are sweeping in, their frosty bite no longer welcome to my feathers. I shiver, and sit, huddling together. I have been in temperate climates for too long. I no longer recognize the invigorating chill that used to come from my homeland.

Some-owl knocks on the door. I don't answer. I'm a prisoner, it's not like I'm supposed to say "come in".

Intyl peeks in, then enters my cell and closes the door behind him with a clunk. His rusty-orange feathers ruffle in the breeze, and he shudders.

"It's cold tonight, isn't it?" Intyl says, trying to put a little cheer in his voice. I turn my head away, and he sighs. He comes closer and sits beside me. "I'm sorry all of this happened." I look at him, wondering if he was as shallow as he sounded.

"My friends died because of all of this," I snarl, "My friend died because I didn't have the strength to hang on. Because I had expended so much energy in escaping. He slipped from my grip, and now he's gone, just like the rest of them." I turn away, so that Intyl didn't see a rebellious tear roll down my feathers. Intyl doesn't look up.

"I don't get how you escaped, those were forged iron shackles. I watched the top blacksmiths make them myself." For once I smile.

"I will not be contained. When I know someone is in danger I will go into a frenzy and you don't want to be near me when that happens." Intyl shakes his head.

"I wouldn't advise you to keep making friends, but you might." I look at him, my mood suddenly curious, but he gets up to leave, and passes through the door without another word. What did he mean by that?

***

I have another visitor. This time it's Byhi, looking bruised but really angry. I consider a taunt, but instead growl deep in my throat, and she hesitates. Then Byhi huffs in anger at her fear and strides toward me.

"What do you want," I growl, a hint of defeat under-laying my tone. Byhi practically radiates the heat of her anger, staring me down with golden eyes.

"I need you for a job," she pouts, a little hesitant in giving me the offer. "The Pauraque asks that you break in one of the new recruits." I raise an eyebrow.

"*You*, the all-powerful owl, need *me*, the lowly prisoner? Am I getting this right?" I mock. Byhi rolls her eyes.

"Be quiet you scrawny little snowflake. I'm not happy about it either." She huffs. Then she comes close, putting her beak in my face and just asking for me to tear her regal mask right off her pretty little face. "But if you try *anything*, your situation will be, let's say, *terminated*, and this offer will no longer stand. Are we clear?" I grin, feeling rebellious.

"As clear as a shining icicle during a break in the blizzard. But I will also make one thing clear. You don't scare me, and the truth is, *you* are afraid of *me*. Your fancy mask and robe are factors meant to suppress, and I'm not entirely convinced that you are a strong as you want me to think."

Byhi screeches for a moment, now completely irate and trying not to wring my neck. "You don't understand your situation. You are not in control here!"

"Maybe I'm not," I admit, "And maybe I don't understand. But I still love driving up your blood-pressure. It's one of the perks of being a wanted prisoner." Byhi screeches again, short and high-pitched.

"You will meet him in the morning," she mutters, and disappears through the door. I smile cruelly. These owls don't understand me. I cannot be contained, nor controlled, nor used for their benefit. My power cannot be harnessed, and I will not go down without a fight. Count on it, Byhi.

Nyk

I screech and thrash, trying to give these soldiers owl a hard time. They miraculously manage to shackle my feet, but that's it. I drive them from my cell, hissing and snapping my beak. They squawk, rushing out.

I hiss once more, and settle down in the far corner, picking at my manacles. They cannot restrain me for long. I won't be chained.

The door opens, and I start to hiss, puffing up my feathers. The lead owl comes in. Byhi. She is careful not to come close, and seems annoyed. Perhaps from a previous conversation. "We will break you," Byhi threats. I snort, chuckling.

"Fool," I laugh, "Like you can tame me. You think I'm some kind of joke? Do you want me to show you what I can do?" Byhi shakes her head, masking her fear.

"Save your breath. We've seen your kind before." Byhi bluffs. I laugh again.

"Oh, you have another snowy owl lying around here somewhere?"

"As a matter of fact," Byhi says coolly, "I do. Guards!" she calls. Two soldiers scurry at her voice. "Bring Arne." Byhi orders. I freeze.

"Arne?" I ask. Now it's Byhi's turn to laugh.

"Don't believe me? You think that you were the wild spirit here, the best of the best? Every owl can be broken. Every last one."

The glow of white feathers starts to show from the shadows outside my door. I walk closer, making no attempt to hide my curiosity even though Byhi seems satisfied by it.

Sure enough, a female snowy owl is pushed in through the doors. She casts poisonous glances at the soldiers, but her shoulder seems slightly limp like it's damaged. She seems tired, but the fire still shines in her eyes. There's no doubt its Arne, the only owl ever to take on a winter wolf and win.

But, what I am equally surprised by was her beauty. Even in this state, she stands with grace and power, with elegance. She is stunning.

Arne locks eyes with mine, and suppresses a gasp. We're both shocked, honestly; we thought we were the only snowy owls here. Surely snowy owls were more powerful than this organization.

"Arne," I breathe. She nods. I blink a couple times; trying to make sure this is real. Byhi laughs, enjoying herself.

"Arne, meet Nyk. Nyk, this is the mighty Arne, our personal mascot." Arne screeches something horrid, the volume shaking the room to its foundations. She thrashes around, making her chains rattle.

"I *belong* to no one, Byhi." Arne snarls. She narrows her eyes, concentrating her fire. Byhi begins to seem nervous, edging away from her.

"I believe we have some unfinished business," Arne threatens. Byhi gulps involuntarily.

"I am in charge here, and will have none of it." Byhi orders, her voice quivering. I'm frozen in place, looking at Arne. They got her. She's their prisoner. If they can capture Arne, what will they do to *me*?

The bravado has been drained from my face, and the thoughts of what they could now do swirl in my head like sharks in the ocean. With this information, this confirmation of their power, *what can they do?* What will they do to me?

Byhi sees my discomfort, and an evil smile crawls up onto her features. "I think he's seen enough." She flicks a claw and the two Great grey owl soldiers start to drag

Arne away. Arne locks eyes with mine once more, and sees what I'm thinking.

"They cannot break us," she calls, "They are as weak as your first impression." Then she's too far to hear. Byhi chuckles again, closing the door behind her.

If they can get to Arne...what is going to happen to me?

But remember what Arne said. They're weak; they just *want* to seem strong.

Still. I'm pretty shaken up.

Chapter 7: Revelation and Betrayal

Nara

"Time to get going," I order. I lift off the ground, and after readjusting for my limp leg, I lead the group through the marsh, careful not to break through the canopy and alert any more soldiers. We weave past vines, and avoid large trees with dangling moss. It's humid and makes me sweat; I like the desert much better.

Kari glides beside me, strong and focused, seemingly ready for anything. She glances at me, looking for leadership. "What is our plan?" Kari asks casually. I understand the real question: *are we going to save Arne again or what?*

"If we are," I say, "Then we're going to need backup. They're growing stronger." Kari nods, recalling the last battle.

"Where are we going to find the help? There aren't many owls capable of taking down Byhi. Arne was probably the last one." Cici prompts. I slow down my flight pattern, straining my memory.

"I know Burrowing owls are hardy fighters, but aren't equipped with the power to take down owls like the Great greys." I think aloud. But then it hits me.

Rhi notices the sparkle in my eye. "No way," she says, shaking her head, "You aren't serious." I grin, despite my throbbing leg.

"Oh, I'm serious alright. Put on your winter coats girls, it's gonna get cold."

Arne

They have captured another snowy owl. I wasn't the only weak one in my species. Maybe there are more powerful owls than what I have fought. Maybe these owls of the Pauraque are more of a threat than I had imagined.

Nyk had been the snowy owl's name. He had seemed shell-shocked, absolutely horrified to see me bound in chains. I'm sure any other owl of my kind would be too; I am infamous among the snowies for my strength and bravery. I am notoriously bold and daring, and known for being unbreakable. To see me as a beaten prisoner...all hope of surviving would be crushed. Because, to Nyk, if I had fallen then everyone was fair game.

The day passes by so slowly. I can't sleep well, and am restless. My wing still aches, though miraculously it is still doing better. Perhaps in about a week I'll be up to full health.

But what then? Do I yet again return to my beloved band of owls? Why do I need to escape...what else do I need to survive for? My goals mean nothing. I don't think I had any goals. I just lived each day, hunting, surviving, thriving. I remember when the Dilecta Arctic was always welcome. Now that I'd spent time in the humid Arko Forest I shivered when its frigid winds kissed my ruffled feathers, and, in truth, I haven't really felt like myself anymore. I try too hard to protect other owls and risk my own life. And when Theo had slipped through my claws...I felt like a failure and a lead weight had lined my wings. Nothing will ever be the same, whether I spend my days here, or with Cici and the others, or back home. Nothing will be right again.

So what do I do here? My new mission is to help the new snowy owl. But what can I do for him? Everything is unclear...

I think like this all day long. When dusk settles into the horizon and finally gives way to the gleaming moon, I'm still thinking, plotting, trying to figure out my plans here. Byhi enters through the door, smiling heartlessly.

She gestures towards my bonds and two soldiers come in, detaching my chains from the wall and gripping them tightly with sharpened talons. "Time for you and Nyk to get to know each other." Byhi hisses.

***

Nyk is in the corner of his cell, his white feathers glowing softly in the darkness like the moonbeams from the hole in the ceiling. Byhi shoves me in, raking her claws against my feathers, the sudden push making me trip over my bonds. They laugh and throw the chains into the room.

Nyk turns from his corner, watching from the shadows. I screech viciously at Byhi and the soldiers and do a mock charge, and they hurriedly close the door, frightened expressions wiping the grins off their faces. I'm satisfied, but now Byhi's scratches bleed, like red stains on a white canvas.

I sigh, and hobble over to the moonlight. I close my eyes for a moment, letting the cold wind flow over my feathers and the soft light bathe my skin. I open them, ending my indulgence, and Nyk is beside me, staring at my new wounds with a sad expression.

"I'm sorry," he whispers. I shake my head.

"I keep my dominance, and it has a minor cost." A pause echoes silence in the room. Nyk searches for the right words to say.

"Why are you here?" he asks. I give some thought to this question, and realize he's asking for the story of how I got captured. I sigh again, my gaze falling to the floor. Nyk sees my expression and starts to back up from his request, but I wave a claw.

"It's fine," I shrug, "It's just a long story." Nyk nods respectfully, and I turn my head once again to the moonlight.

"I'm sure you've heard of my reputation," I begin, "Of fighting winter wolves and fending off rival owls. They're true. But none of those things could help me make sense of when a Eurasian Eagle owl starting chasing me from the arctic.

"When we reached Arko, she proceeded to try and catch me by grabbing my shoulder." I shudder, and look at my shoulder, the pain becoming all too real. "I bit her claw and got away but fell to the forest below and was badly hurt.

"Two burrowing owls, sisters called Nara and Cici, found me, and Cici persuaded Nara to help me. This inspired a Saw-whet owl, Kari, to help as well. Kari has always been...undecided. It was a big step for her.

"After some misunderstandings, they eventually helped me try and recover. But within the first day we knew something was afoot. Nara and Kari were on patrol when they saw the soldiers." Nyk comes closer, drinking in every detail. I lower my head from the light, and continue. "Kari was lagging behind when she was caught by them. They had a little Northern hawk owl too. He was Theo. Cici, Kari, and Nara were able to take care of the first round, and I'd had around three days of rest. But that's when my mindset changed. I went from survivalist to protector.

"When the second round came, my group was captured. Rikki had led the attack. I was needed, and from then on I've strained my wing. I did save my band of owls, and sent Rikki spiraling to the forest below. We had stopped to rest when Rikki's accomplice, Celfina, ambushed us." My eyes dart around, as I relive the moment.

"That was how they captured you?" Nyk asks, sounding almost unimpressed.

"No," I clarify, "They had a hold of Cici." I close my eyes. "I gave myself up for her. They tried to make me a soldier, but I just got wilder and more desperate. I escaped with another owl who was to become a soldier."

"Rhi, the barn owl," Nyk breathes. I nod. "But...the shackles..."

"Broke them," I answer simply. Nyk looks at me with astonishment, and my mood grows almost serious. "When you finally care about other owls and have someone to protect, you will do anything to get back to them. The iron cuffs were just another obstacle that I had overcome."

"Rhi and I were heading back to where I had last seen my group when I realized that Cici would've persuaded them to rescue me by that time. I had no idea how many nights had passed.

"So we turned back, and managed to help the group. There was a big battle, and I finally knew what happened to all my adversaries." Nyk's eyes widen, hungry for the next piece in my story.

"Rikki hadn't died, and Celfina was as psychotic as ever. But the Eurasian eagle owl that had chased me...she now wore a silver mask. Byhi had become second in command in this assault.

"I tried to take them all on, rotating between battles, but Rikki took me down, and then Celfina joined us. We were falling towards the Worte Marsh, and they tightened my grip. If they were going down, I was going to die with them. Somehow I wiggled free and went to the battle above. But all my friends were dead."

Nyk studies me curiously. "But that wasn't it," he says.

"They're all dead! How is there more to this story?" I shout, turning away. Nyk presses on, coming over so he could look into my downcast eyes.

"They're not all dead, are they?" He presses. I look up at him, all of a sudden angry and hurt.

"Why should I tell you?" I bait.

"I guess you don't have to, there's no reason to." Nyk says, shrugging. I sigh.

"You understand that anything said beyond this point could get me or whatever surviving owls mentioned killed or worse?"

Nyk nods solemnly.

"Well I couldn't get free. And they're not all dead.

"I called for help then. I knew I wouldn't live another day if I didn't have help fending off these suicide owls. The only one who had a spare wing was Theo, and he was the jokester of the group. But he came to me anyway, and bit the claws of Rikki and Celfina hard. But when we were about to hit a tree down in the marsh, he slipped through my claws." I pause, fighting back some tears. "Then he was gone. Nara, Cici, and Kari came back to regroup, but the soldiers were on our tail. So I gave myself up, and drew them away. I let them have me. I told them everyone was dead. They might as well be. Cici probably hates me because she loved Theo, and Nara probably hates me because she loves Cici more than anything."

Nyk nods again, this time sympathetic. "I'm sorry all this happened." His gaze rests on my damaged wing. I spread my wings, wincing slightly, and flap a couple times, creating some wind in the room.

"Like I said, it hasn't healed, but I'll fly with it." I comment. I focus on Nyk, and realize that he needs my help. "You're beginning to understand the power of this place, aren't you?" I ask meaningfully. Nyk stays silent.

"You're supposed to be the strongest of the owls," he says, rising up his own wings, "And if you can go down here, then how am I going to stay alive."

"I'll do what I can," I promise. "Though I'll say that you cannot make attachments here. I have learned that it is dangerous, and has consequences. Even outside of here, it's dangerous. Then again, I'm still breathing, so it must be okay." I pause.

"How did they get you?" I ask.

"I had run into a winter wolf," Nyk explains, "And I was an easy target."

"They always come when you're weak," I agree. "But don't forget who you are. The reason why they got you after a battle with a winter wolf was because they couldn't handle you if you were at full health. We're dangerous to them, and they're afraid of us."

Nyk agrees. "We are *snowy owls*." I hold out a claw.

"The Snowy Alliance?" I propose.

"The Snowy Alliance," Nyk confirms. A flame flickers across our eyes, determination and new-found strength invigorating us.

The door bursts open, Byhi smiling dangerously. "I hope you've gotten to know each other, because your first training begins now."

Nyk

Arne and I are led down the hall, shifting shadows dancing across the brown dirt walls. Large soldiers walk both in front and behind us, watching our every move under copper masks.

Arne is right. They *do* fear us.

The cramped dirt passage opens up to a high-ceilinged cave. We're led deeper into the room, faint echoes whispering in my ear. The space seems to be made of rough gray rock, and there's a single pillar of rock in the center of the room. Two white barn owls gently perch on it; they look calm, slightly graceful, and eerie.

"The Twin Wings," Arne whispers. The Twin Wing's characteristic glowing emerald eyes blink for a second, dilating as they focus on us.

"The two snowy owls," Pyre starts.

"Joined together by resentment of their captors and the bond of their species," Ruole finishes.

"Byhi," they warn, "Do not let them have reasons to dislike your rule." Then they turn back to their apparent mission. "Training," they declare, "Will begin."

"Keep in mind," Pyre says.

"That this could be life or death. They will not hold back," Ruole finishes. Before Arne or I could open our beaks, twenty Great grey and Short-eared soldier owls pour in behind us.

Now, it would've been easier if they had removed our chains. But they hadn't. And I'm pretty sure they did that on purpose.

We fly up, beating our mighty wings to get to about halfway up the chamber. The soldier owls follow us and we get to work, slashing and dodging, knocking the masks off our enemies. I don't think those owls are even soldiers anymore. More like relentless owl-zombies. Their eyes are slightly glazed as if bright light was still reflecting off of them.

At first everything is fine. But I falter. I am fighting an owl in front of me when another soldier clipps my wings from behind. I loose control, just for that one second. The two soldiers take their chance and send me spiraling to the ground. I wince as I try to straighten out, but I am going to fall on my back.

Arne screeches for a moment, finishing off the owls she was fighting, and dives for me. The intense tenacity of trying to reach me showed through Arne's eyes, the inferno of battle-rage giving her an edge. She clasps my foot and tries to fly up, slowing my decent. The weight of the iron chains doesn't help either, and we are still falling fast. I can almost feel the cold impact of the rocky ground below.

We're only a few feet away now, and Arne closes her eyes, gritting her beak, straining against the drag and using all her might. With a final grunt I land with only a soft thud, and Arne collapses on the ground.

Her wing is damaged again because of you, I scold myself. *How is she going to defend herself?*

The two owls that had clipped me let themselves fall from the altitude, preparing to finish us off. I slowly roll over onto my feet, and jump up and lash out at them when they have come close enough. Then all of us are on the ground, and I skip around, avoiding their blows. My vision is blurry, but my mark is true. A few blows and carefully aimed jabs and the two soldier owls have joined their comrades in unconsciousness.

Arne is finally to her feet, and we're both breathing heavily. Out of the corner of my eye I see Byhi leave the chamber, extremely terrified of our power, with the Twin Wings smiling at her actions and shaking their heads in unison like the disc on a grandfather clock.

"You have earned a few days' rest," they declare, and they seem as if they are more kind than other owls who have authority over us. They seem like they care about each individual a little more.

I nod gratefully, and two Great greys fly in, grabbing our chains and dragging us along. Arne stands tall, focusing ahead. She grits her beak again, carefully taking each step. I know exactly what she's doing because I've done it before.

They approach my cell door and stop. "The Pauraque has approved that you two will be staying together." A voice says from behind us. Arne and I turn to see Intyl, solemn as always. He glances at Arne as if he knew what we had to do and was trying to say, *I'm sorry I couldn't have helped you*, and then gestures to the soldiers to lock us up.

As they chain us to the wall, Arne remains stiff, glaring at them. Once all the owls are gone and they close the door behind them, I reach out to catch Arne. Her eyes roll back into her head for a moment and her legs buckle. She grunts softly, conscious again once she almost hits the ground. I help her sit up against the wall, and I shake my head.

"I was stupid. I had tunnel vision, and was only focusing on the owl in front of me," I mutter. Arne disagrees.

"As the Twin Wings said, it's just another step in training. In each fight you find your weaknesses and turn them into strengths. I overexert myself, and then when it matters that I have the strength, I don't," Arne sighs. "That's what I need to work on. Otherwise, next time it'll be worse for me." She catches my stare at her wing.

"If only I had the time to let it heal," she says, "Then I'd be a lot less vulnerable than I am now. Hopefully these few days will be enough." I nod, silent.

If I don't step up then she's the one that will die next time, I remind myself. *So I better step it up.*

Kari

Once Nara told us to put on our winter coats I knew exactly what she was planning. "Oh Owls. You're kidding me!" I groan. "Am I the only one with common sense here?" Rhi puts her claws up in defeat.

"You think *I* like it? I'm with you Kari." Rhi says, shaking her head with a small smile on her face. Cici's eyes widen as she sees what we're talking about.

"This is our last chance," Nara says softly. Cici's expression hardens to that of stone, a cold, uncaring expression that sends chills down my spine. This isn't the Cici that I met, the one who ordered us to help Arne. This isn't the one that flew into battle with the soldier owls to save me and Theo, that laughed at Theo's jokes like they were the only two in the world.

Theo. An owl with a sparkle in his eye and a joke always the first thing out of his beak. Gone. He took Cici's innocence and happiness too. Now she is just like the rest of us. All grown up. Hard and determined. Cici is no longer naïve of what could happen to an owl.

"Let's go," Cici says, flying ahead.

***

"I was never built for this weather! Owls it's c-c-c-*cold*!" I yell over the gale, more to myself than to anyone in particular.

The icy winds sting my face like a thousand needles. The shards of snow whistle past my ears and block out any sound, drowning everything out with its constant roar. Cici and Nara gasp and struggle for each breath in front of me. They're built for the desert. Sure, the desert gets below freezing at night but they'd be safe and toasty inside their burrows by then.

Rhi fights against the gusts, eyes almost completely shut, snow stuck on the top of her feathers. We're like ragdolls in the whipping blizzard, completely at the mercy of the storm. I don't know what we'll do if we don't find those owls. I'll tear my feathers out if I had to endure this for nothing.

The Dilecta Arctic is unforgiving. It's icy just like its landscape. I thought the biggest peril of this journey was finding the snowies, but battling the weather will be the most challenging thing yet. I doubt there is anything that can compare to it.

"We had better find them!" I shout. I can barely make out Nara's nod in reply. Luckily I'm downwind so I manage to catch most of her response.

"The snowies...advantage...worth it...Arne...saved,"

"I'm just saying," I mutter, keeping the rest of my complaints to myself.

Once again my old mindset turns on, like a radio flickering in and out of a long-forgotten station. The Fate owl's punishment, maybe that's what this is. No forest owl should ever have to endure this.

I glance out into the wind, trying to make out horizon. We've been flying day and night, taking a few rests here and there. The sun is supposed to be burning brightly, but it can't be seen because of all the snow ripping past. Nothing can be seen.

Yet the snow seems to be bending around something off to my right. I squint to try and make what is out there, but all I see is a field of white, like snowy interference.

Rhi catches my gaze and her eyes widen as she spots the figure. "Nara! Cici!" she yells at the top of her lungs. They barely catch her words, turning around and now hovering beside us. They see it too.

"Something's there," Nara breathes. I nod.

"I think we found our snowie!" Rhi shrieks as it bolts toward us, yellow claws materializing out of the endless white. The snowy owl's yellow eyes pop out from the colorless world, focusing on me. He dives and tackles me with his talons, the freezing snow rising up to meet me.

On impact, it starts to melt, creeping into my feathers, spreading its cold virus throughout my small frame.

Despite his scrutinizing gaze, I keep my cool (which isn't hard surrounded by snow) and stare back, surprisingly calm. He seems to see through me, and backs off from his offensive nature.

The other three land, my group standing off to the side to make it clear they weren't surrounding him. "We need a place to stay, and we need your help. A few of your fellow owls have been captured. We're trying to get them back." Nara explains, gingerly holding up her right leg so it doesn't touch the snow. He looks us over, and decides we aren't a threat.

"Come with me," he orders. He pauses for a moment, growling deep in his throat, but his curiosity wins out, and turns away to lead us to a pile of rocks in the distance. Frost covers them, but it seems dark in the center, as if there is a room inside the shelter.

The Destiny Owl has a plan for us. It's a very interesting one to say in the least.

Arne

I feel inadequate. My wing is holding me back. It's healed considerably, but Byhi was cruel and said that today was my last day of rest. So close to full health until they make me strain it again and my progress backpedals.

Nyk acts as if he's done it before. Most of us snowy owls have. We don't show weakness, and hide our strengths for surprise attacks. Swift, silent, and you're done. That's how our plans are executed. That's how our *prey* is executed.

"We need to get out of here," Nyk says, breaking the silence. He's staring up at the moon wistfully, trying to formulate a plan that will allow him to finally fly next to it again. I want to shake my head, but restrain the action.

"There is no way out," I sigh. Nyk turns, desperation edging his features.

"But *you've* done it," he says quickly. Now I cannot hold it in, and shake my head, realizing how defeated I am.

"It's only a temporary relief," I explain, "Escape is only a mental comfort. You can never forget this place. And you can never stay out of here for long."

"You sound like Celfina!" Nyk shouts. He looks like he wants to rip his feathers out, growling in frustration as he paces the room. "If we can't escape, then we'll survive this place," he says to himself, "We'll rise to the top, we'll..." I tune his rant out, preferring to sort out my priorities.

Why don't I care about my group anymore? Theo's death was hard, but why did it change me this much? I know I failed. But has it really driven me to giving up completely? Nyk needs someone to look up to. I have to be the owl that can help him get out of here.

Then what? Is that what I want to do? Save Nyk like I did Rhi? I've never been this undecided in my whole hunting career.

"Why have you given up?" Nyk whines, interrupting my thoughts. I look up at him, sighing.

"I've gone from a renowned free-spirit to a vulnerable owl. I was unable to help *myself*. I changed then, to a protector. Then I was captured, and made prisoner. Now

I'm a failure. Now *I'm* the baggage here! Excuse me if I'm a little undecided on what I'm going to become next."

"But..." Nyk protests.

"What do you *want* me to be?" I shout. Before Nyk could answer Intyl once again barges through the door.

"It's time for training," he says, breathless. We both stand, but Intyl shakes his head. "Just Arne. Nyk, you're going to spend some time with Byhi."

Byhi walks into the room, smiling viciously. Two Great greys start to unhook my chains. I silently comply with them, letting them start to drag me to training. What was I supposed to do? But then Nyk screeches, and pulls at his chain desperately.

"No," Nyk orders, "I'm not leaving her." Byhi chuckles slightly, trying to mask her annoyance. "As if you have a choice," she croons.

Nyk screeches once more, and pushes past the guards, standing beside me. He stares Byhi down, cold and unmoving. "I'm not leaving her." I smile slightly, trying to be strong for him, but then it hits me.

He isn't worried about Byhi, he's worried about me. And what will happen when I go to training alone.

I'm stunned.

"Move it!" a guard says, and gives a crippling blow to my damaged wing. I scream, and crumple to the floor, trying to catch my breath. Nyk goes berserk, screeching and throwing aside the Great greys. "No!" Nyk protectively throws his wings over me, shielding me from the soldiers. "No!" He forcefully screams, daring the guards to try and provoke him.

Byhi is stunned at Nyk's actions. I would be too, but it is all I can do to keep myself together. Nyk stands above me, an adrenaline rush pumping through him. He was truly enraged. Over something they did to me.

How far did he secretly care about me?

"Tomorrow, then," Byhi says cautiously, eyeing Nyk curiously. The guards leave, and soon only Nyk and I are in the room.

Nyk immediately bends over to inspect me. "Are you okay? I won't let them do that again, if they touch so much as one feather then..."

"I'm fine," I croak, slowly rising from the floor. He supports me gently, ready to catch me at any moment. I take a moment to look into his eyes, and I wonder how he managed to scare Byhi so badly as to leave. What had Byhi seen in him?

"No you're not," Nyk says softly, and guides me to the center of the room, moonlight starting to shine down from the ceiling. We sit and bathe in the moonlight, longing to fly under its watchful eye once again, to feel the wind ruffle our feathers.

"I want you to be happy," Nyk whispers. At first I don't know what he's talking about, the statement coming out of the blue. Then I remember our conversation before the guards barged in. I let my gaze fall a little, but Nyk uses a claw to gently lift up my beak. "All I want is for you to be happy. If freedom is what makes you happy, what makes your heart sing, then we'll escape together. If saving these owls is what you're called to do, then we'll fight and we'll free them."

I finally bring my eyes up to Nyk. "It feels like I've lost everything. It's not that I've given up, it's just I don't know what to do with myself."

"Then help me," Nyk pleads, his eyes edged with fear, "I can't do this alone. I don't want to spend the rest of my life here. But I won't leave without you either if you are condemned here." He holds out a claw. "The Snowy Alliance?"

My emotions settle within me, and the confusion is driven out. I take his claw. "The Snowy Alliance."

As the ribbons of orange sunlight pierce the sky, shattering our hopeful night, I come closer to Nyk, perching beside him. Nyk looks at me, surprised, and I close my eyes. Nyk settles closer, and we perch beside each other, trying to drown out the thoughts of tomorrow's training.

***

"Remember," Nyk tells me, the stars starting to blink into view, "You're not alone." Then the wooden door bursts open, with Intyl and a bunch of Great greys as our visitors.

"Nyk," he says, "You've been called." Nyk takes one hopeful glance at me, then waits as the soldiers take his chains and lead him out of the room. As the soldiers disappear, two more come to take me.

"You'll be going to the Unveiling," Intyl informs me, almost stuttering. His rusty orange feathers flutter slightly in the breeze from the ceiling.

The soldiers once again remove my chains, and I'm lead away, heading down the dirt passage once more. Intyl tries to look at me apologetically, but I just blink once and turn my head away. I don't want to talk right now.

I file into the crowd, once again in the room where the Twin Wings chose me to be a soldier. This time, the rocky ledge is empty of authority.

All the owls in the sea of the captured whisper cautiously, anxiously awaiting what owl might step out onto the ledge. The name "the Unveiling" was ominous enough. Something big was going to happen here.

A large screech makes all of us jump, and a large owl flies up to the ledge to claim her spot. Intyl launches himself up into the air, going to join her.

Byhi stares down onto us, as if we were simply ants underneath her, worthless and deserving no thought. She tries to wear a regal prowess, the aura of her cool nature unsettling all of us.

"I am Lady Byhi," she booms, "Your new queen. From now on you'll answer to *me*. All internal affairs will be passed by me and any conspiracies shall reach my ears. But do not be afraid. I shall govern with wisdom and I will work diligently to reach my ultimate goal of improving your conditions, eventually linking all of you into one, big, nation!" Hesitantly and out of fear, the crowd cheers, though there's no heart in it.

Byhi continues, unhindered. "The Pauraque has allowed me to assemble meetings such as these in emergencies, and all of you shall be informed of our current status, as you are now part of the network and deserve to know what is going on, do you not?" Everyone nods, looking at each other. A few of the wiser ones see the trick, and close any doors that lead to an open mind, seeing through her political lies.

"We shall prosper, and grow stronger by the day! We will rise as one of the most powerful nations of all time! You will be heroes, whether in our patriotic army or at base. The name of Lady Byhi will be known to everyone, and the Pauraque shall be made great! We will achieve ultimate luxury and cohesiveness, working together to build a strong, superior realm that could compare to no other!" The owls that nodded earlier cheer more openly now. Compared to the hardships endured here, luxury seems like an unattainable goal. But it's something worth hoping for, like a mouse dangled in front of them.

"For the Pauraque! For Lady Byhi!" Byhi prompts.

"For the Pauraque! For Lady Byhi! Lady Byhi!" the owls cheer. What a pack of fools, cheering for their slavery-masters. As if Byhi cared whether they lived or died. Fools.

Intyl nods and cheers, and Byhi flies off the ledge, disappearing behind me. Once she leaves his smile drops and he seems annoyed and sad, frustrated with his own self. Then he follows her, leaving me to wonder.

If Intyl doesn't like Byhi, then how many others have not succumbed to her lies?

...but more importantly...is there hope that not all these owls have been brainwashed?

Rhi

I hate the snow. I never want to come back here. I can't wait to get out of here, and actually see the moon, and bathe myself in its soft, silvery, almost-blue glow.

The snowy owl leads us to the pile of rocks, and down a tunnel. It's quite odd. I didn't know that snowy owls could dig. Or maybe this was like a bunker for them during the blizzards. That might make sense.

The short corridor leads to a large room, obviously hand-dug. It seems like finer work, so he couldn't have done it. I would ponder further but once we're inside he looks at us expectantly, waiting for our story.

I feel as though I'm the one best qualified for the job. I step forward. "My name is Rhi," I begin, "And ever since I was an owlet I've been a slave to a bird called the Pauraque and her followers. They're preparing to take over all of Argon, and have kidnapped one of your kind."

The snowy owl raises his eyebrows in disbelief, but I continue. "Arne was captured and is still in captivity, and we need your help to take down the organization. If it is really as powerful as to detain Arne, think of what it can do."

The snowy owl nods respectfully. "Everyone knows Arne. To think that there are birds strong enough to take her on...I hate to think about it. Arne was...untouchable, and if she can be captured, then anyone can." He shakes his head sorrowfully, then glances at us and quickly straightens. Apparently all snowy owls are the same; trying to hide what they feel, whether it's physical or mental.

"This is Kari," I introduce, gesturing to the Saw-whet owl, "And Nara and Cici."

"We used to have a Northern Hawk owl named Theo in our group," Cici says, staring at the snowy owl with cold determination, "But he was killed by some followers of the Pauraque." The snowy owl doesn't seem to care about Theo's death—what was he to him anyway, he never knew him—but is taken aback at Cici's attitude.

"I thought Burrowing owls were more upbeat," he remarks. Cici shrugs.

"I used to be. But you won't be nice once you experience what the Pauraque does," Cici says.

"I see your point," the snowy owl says gravely. "Well, obviously I won't be enough. I'll rally the others, that is, if you're telling the truth. You do know that this is quite a tale to believe, isn't it?"

Cici steps forward, and so do I. I take my turn, looking him in the eye. "Try me. All I can remember is work, work, and more work, long nights and sleepless days, my talons sore from polishing battle-masks. You want to know what it is like?"

Now Cici draws the snowy owl's attention, seizing her chance to share her story. "At first I wanted to help every owl, and skipped around picking desert flowers. I started seeing owls getting hurt and I was a wreck. I thought that having a sore wing was bad. Arne has almost permanently damaged hers, running away from them and saving us while she's at it. What do you think happened when Theo died during a battle with some soldiers of the Pauraque?" Cici dares. The snowy owl says nothing, his wisdom and his own version of her experiences silently telling us the answer. "I want revenge for Theo by freeing Arne, and whether you help us or not I'm going to march in there and take her back."

"Strong words for such a small owl," the snowy owl comments. He takes a deep breath. "As a snowy owl I had early exposure, and had the wisdom of my parent's understandings passed down to me. Rhi, the feeling in your words and Cici's disposition is proof enough. I have heard stories of this Pauraque's activities, and it all makes sense. I will be right back." The snowy owl starts to head back the way we came when I stop him.

"Wait!" I plead. He turns to look at me, curious at what would make me delay him. "I haven't even gotten your name." The snowy owl pauses, considering.

"Tyrn," he answers, and then he's gone, once more out into the arctic gale.

"Do you think this is going to work?" I ask quietly, turning towards Nara. Nara has taken the role of being our leader, so I have looked to her for decisions.

She pauses, eyes searching the ground, looking a little tired. "I don't know, but this is our best shot at taking down Byhi and the Pauraque."

"Tyrn," Kari whispers to herself, "Tyrn to turn the tide of the war."

Tyrn

What am I supposed to think of these owls?

Being a snowy owl, I am not one to make friends by nature. I trust no one. But when Rhi came up to me and told me of her life as a slave, she was either really determined to execute her plan to trap me or she really *had* lived a hard life. And the first conclusion was certainly possible because any owl that challenges a snowie has to be partially out of its mind in the first place.

The arctic wind blasts onto my face as I leave the protection of the burrow. I vaguely remember my parents and how they chose my name. My name sounded like a cross between the words "tear" and "turn". I learned some wisdom from my parents, but also found a lot of knowledge from experience. I can analyze well, and when I looked at Rhi, I saw the lines of worry and exhaustion, of years of hopelessness and unending labor. There is nothing that could replicate that look but of slavery. This little owl was speaking the truth.

And the attitude of Cici was perfect, something very stereotypical after enduring something like the situation she described. At first she was carefree and naïve, and when she saw what the world was really like she became like us; she became hardened of brazened metal with her bite just as cold, determination of revenge just as scarred into her hunger of goals. It is a condition that is irreversible, and it melds into a part of who you are. Again, this is another thing that sold me, something that cannot be faked.

So I trudged through the snow, finding some solid ground before I take off. As I finally lift my feet from the ground I feel calm. I am in my own domain and am perfectly safe here, in the middle of a blizzard. It makes me feel alive.

I rip off an earsplitting screech, something that penetrats through the storm and resonates far and wide. They will be here alright. I'm an owl fairly known; I am nowhere near as famous as Arne, but the few that know me have respect. I have a tendency for figuring out the truth in things, and when serious matters are at hand, all snowy owls turn to me. Like I am their wise leader.

I shift my course for the Glacier. The Burrow and the Glacier are the two meeting places, (neither were created by us) and since I wanted to speak with the others privately before they met the strange group of owls, I chose the Glacier.

The Glacier is a large iceberg that provides some cover from the storm, and a few frozen trees that have long-since died formed a ring directly beneath it, creating the perfect spot to perch and discuss important matters concerning the freedom of our species. We are solitary most of the time, very true, but we aren't fools. When a meeting is called you attended, no matter how free-spirited you are. Because sometimes it isn't all about you, and you'd best be in the loop when a big threat arises.

The Glacier fringes the horizon, glowing a clear blue with what little sunlight shows through the snowstorm. Already I see snowy ghosts heading for it, completely invisible expect for the slight disturbance in how the snow fell.

The gray, gnarled branches loom in front of me, and I swoop smoothly, landing with a crunch on the snow-covered perch. Two, three, four more land near me. A few more land and now we numbered around twenty. Of course, there are rumored to be more, but we could never find them. No bird could.

Twenty sets of golden eyes peer at me. Some are curious, others slightly annoyed; a few are nervous because meetings are maybe called once every few years, and a couple owls simply stare on, believing that this is totally unimportant compared to their daily schedules.

"The Snowy Ghosts," I boom, "I have some very important news." Many owls shift on their perch. When someone says they have important news it's always a bad sign. I clear my throat and continue. "I'm sure you've all heard the rumors." Many nods ripple through the crowd.

"But let me solidify your fears that they are true." Of course, in a normal crowd of birds, there would be many gasps, but we were snowy owls and we are usually unperturbed with many things...usually *dangerous*, things.

"I myself have gained some scars a while back from some soldier owls. The whispers of a bird called the Pauraque have matched with my encounter. Although this is hardly evidence, I have met a group of birds you will want to meet. They have experienced first-hand of the Pauraque's operation, and seek our help to bring it down."

"Yes, this could be a threat to us Tyrn," a young and wise female agrees, "But what is the specific threat? We aren't protectors of all owls. We number so few."

I pause, taking a couple breaths. "We have every right to be concerned. Do you all remember Arne?" Almost every owl's eyes widen at this.

"Tyrn," the female asks cautiously, "You're not saying that...she's fallen to these birds, are you?" I close my eyes for a moment, and it seals the effect.

"According to these owls, Arne has indeed been captured."

"We need to go see them," someone says.

"No, let them come to us," another suggests.

"We must go to the Burrow where I have placed them currently. There is one Saw-whet owl, a Barn owl, and two Burrowing owls. All have testimonies, and I believe that you'll see how the facts fit." I say. Many owls nod, and we all take off, flying towards the Burrow.

Nara

I'm exhausted, but also slightly apprehensive. They have to believe us. These owls are the only chance of bringing down the organization. They refuse and no owl can stop the Pauraque.

Rhi paces. I can feel her pain. Rhi's putting everything on the line...I can't imagine being a slave all my life. She has to tell them her life story to sell it; she has to dredge up all those awful memories.

Cici growls slightly, finally plopping down on the ground. I can barely recognize her now. So angry and resentful. She's no longer a little owlet.

And Kari, she's so silent and strong. She went from a nervous wreck, an owl who couldn't decide if she wanted to go right or left, to a fly or stay put. Now she's a silent warrior. Kari hovers by my side, just slightly tensed. Although Rhi's new to the group, I can't recognize the old Cici or Kari. They just aren't the same anymore.

What have I done to Cici? When I let us plunge out into the sandstorm instead of trying to go back to the burrow, was that my fatal decision? Perhaps I let Cici's compassion get in the way of what was best for her. I don't think she grew right through this journey. Theo's d...disappearance has been hard on her. He was the one owl that could truly make her happy.

So what have I done to help? I was so focused on planning our next move to rescue Arne when Theo was alive; I thought that getting Arne back would make Cici happy. But did she really need me more then, compared to how I was constantly at the charts, plotting a rescue mission? I thought that would make her happy. Or at least I thought...maybe I thought wrong.

Sleep tries to grab me, but I'm still trying to figure everything out. Could I have tried harder to be Cici's mom? To look after her, and not do everything out of love to protect her? I don't think she liked the whole warrior thing.

Kari sees me lulling in and out, and nods to me. "Get some rest. I'll keep watch for when Tyrn comes back." I smile gratefully, and let myself slip away.

Nyk

I leave with a couple of Great greys. That's all I've seen around here, just the Great grey owls and the Short-eared. I've caught glances of some Bay owls, but they aren't suited for a job like me. I'm big. So they need big owls.

I'm led into a small room of gray rock, just like every other room. It has a low ceiling, and contains a single grungy and cracked mirror. They shove me in and close the door.

The room is empty except for the mirror. No one's here. Maybe they're coming later, and I'm supposed to wait.

Sure enough, it isn't long before the metal door once again creaks open. I turn, and come face to face with an extremely beautiful owl. The Eurasian Eagle owl looks at me coolly, the aura of her authority obviously speaking for itself.

"I am Byhi," she says. The snowy owl instinct inside of me immediately flashes red lights. Owls of authority are dangerous here. She strides in, a richly purple robe flowing gracefully behind her. Her claws click on the rocky floor and echo, and the lustrous golden pin on her robe sparkles in the low light. What is most eye-catching is her shining silver battle mask.

"I will be your new queen," Byhi says, as if she were simply telling me yesterday's news. I blink, half-surprised at this new information. My cautiousness quickly takes over.

"Why are you here," I demand. Byhi clicks her tongue unhappily.

"That is no way to talk to your new queen," Byhi chides. She looks me over, her eyes radiating solid confidence and utter control. "I've heard you have potential." I don't answer. What is there to say? This is obviously a dangerous owl.

Byhi walks around me, leisurely inspecting me. "I know you were a little cocky at first, but that has burnt off. What I see is a beautiful, strong-and-silent warrior, who speaks with his actions and not his words. A careful owl, loyal to the end of his days." I shiver slightly. She's describing that small part of me, the part that has been unnecessary to my life for so long that it's almost been erased from my personality completely. *How does she know me?*

Byhi locks eyes with mine, as if reading my thoughts. "The reason why I have risen to such a high position is that I'm the best of the best. I see weaknesses and can either exploit them or make them your strengths. You can either work with me or against me; but everyone knows that they do not want to cross me." She pauses, then backs off.

"The masks' color is very important. The silver is the highest you'll ever see. Bronze are the top commanders of the operation. Brasses are very important, but have to answer to someone. And copper, they're just plain old soldiers. You..." she turns her head to the side for a moment, then steps closer.

Byhi's voice changes, but I realize it isn't her. There was another bird in the room. Some-bird had entered without a sound.

In the most tempting, alluring, and irresistible voice full of poisonous desire, I hear the Pauraque whisper "...do you want to be a bronze?"

Arne

I let the wind ruffle my feathers, huddled in the corner, the two iron chains wrapped around my ankles like tireless coiled snakes. Not that there is anything wrong with snakes. They make *really* good mid-day snacks.

I hear the door swing open again, but there is no laugh of the soldiers. Slowly, talons scrape along the floor, and eventually stop beside me. I know who it is, but I don't move. I'm tired.

"I'm sorry," Nyk says softly, putting some benite moss on some of my bad scratches. I finally look up, and my expression darkens. In the growing dawn, I see the twinkle of a bronze metal-mask. He sees my expression and opens his beak to explain, but I turn away, closing my eyes again.

"Go kill some more owls. Maybe you can capture more that were just like us." I whisper. Nyk gives up, saddened, and walks away, disappearing like a ghost from the fading shadows. A single rebellious tear rolls down my feathers.

He will join the fallen owls. There is no longer any hope of a single owl escaping the lies.

Why Nyk? Why him? He almost had me. He made me let down my guard. Then...he turns. Why Nyk?

I fly up the cone-shaped ceiling and corkscrew through the opening at the top. Tears flow more freely now, as the true betrayal of Nyk's actions set in. The night air rushes to meet me, the cold nip of the Dilecta winds greeting me warmly. Well, technically, *coldly*, since it feels like it blankets me in ice.

I remember the voices in the wind. I remember meeting Rhi, and now, by the sound of her voice, I know that it was her, searching for someone in the night mists. She seemed to be the type that tried to give hope to other owls, to give them something to hold onto. I'm sure that was it. She seemed to know no one else, and only had ties to the captured owls in general.

Maybe I should carry on the tradition.

So, with that thought, I give a mighty screech, something full of power and an undefeatable energy, something invigorating. In response, I hear a few more distant screeches, joining my call for the greats. I have to try and see if they'll resist. Whoever makes it through, I'll save. I'll give them that.

A soft "hello" hadn't seemed appropriate for the state these owls were in. They needed some battle-adrenaline to pull them through. Give them a beat to march to.

So I screech again. Now there are dozens of owls making a choir of screeches, resounding answers that proclaim a rebellion. As my screech dies away, I smile. I will lead them to victory against Byhi and the Pauraque. That's what I want to do.

That's...that's what will make me happy.

Chapter 8: Plans To Fight and Conquer

Nyk

I cannot stand seeing Arne like this. What's worse is now, in her eyes, I'm a traitor and have joined the ones who cannot be saved. I'm hopeless.

So as I turn away, with no soldiers to monitor me, I have to keep my plan straight, and not let my feelings get in the way of my position. Arne doesn't know what I am planning, and so I have to stand against whatever she thinks of me to pull it off.

I walk back down the hall alone, the flickering light of the torches the only source of heat in the subzero corridors. A few guards pass me, not giving a second glance. I am of high authority now, I'm higher up than even Celfina or Rikki or any other brass lieutenants. No one can challenge me now.

As I continue to stride back to the war room, my mind wanders. I wonder about Arne's old group. Are they really still alive? If so, could they pose a threat to the Pauraque and her base here at Opus?

What about poor little Theo? Is he really dead? And Arne didn't tell me everything. The surviving soldiers told us that Arne killed Celfina and Rikki. They told us that a little traitorous barn owl defeated Byhi too, and they thought she was still alive, but I managed to convince them that they had died afterwards from exhaustion and wounds. That they had succumbed to death right after they won.

I had somehow kept them quiet. But not for long. I don't have much time. My era of free reign will come to an end soon. Nothing lasts for long here.

I turn right, into a brightly lit room with a single slab of rock in the center. Byhi awaits me, in full costume. Her silver masks glitters in the torchlight, and Intyl stands nervously beside her. At the head of the table, there is a perch shrouded in shadows, with the outline of a small ruffled bird sitting on it.

"Nyk," Byhi coos, "You made it." Intyl nods in agreement, then goes back to staring blankly at the rocky slate.

"You are essential to our plan," the Pauraque says smoothly, "And it was crucial that you attended." She gestures to Byhi.

"Let us begin, shall we?" Byhi prompts as she pulls out a large scroll. Byhi carefully unrolls it onto the rock, and elaborate pictures and maps become clear on the parchment. Around the edges of the map are four rattlesnakes, hissing poisonously with their rattles vibrating. It looks so alive, as if they were doing it right now.

The map depicts all of Argon, our known world. Starting from the top, we have Dilecta Arctic. A sketched tunnel labeled "the Burrow" and a ring of trees and a large mountain of ice are dubbed "the Glacier". I repress a gasp. No one but a snowy owl should know the location of the Burrow and the Glacier. But, in the far right corner, the arctic fades away, the letters "unexplored" floating around its borders like a wisp of inky smoke.

Going clockwise, then there was the Worte Marsh. In scrawled letters, the word "UNKNOWN" covers the entire space. Nothing much there.

At the bottom of the map, the Bleia Desert seeps in, its sands like a golden ocean, lapping at the borders of the

Worte Marsh and the Arko Forest. In the center, the word "populated" is all that is there.

At the center left is the Arko Forest. Its border with the Bleian Desert is called in cursive letters, "the Rhodes of Time". Farther, in the deep of the forest, it says "Hunting Grounds". It must mean that there are a lot of owls to capture there.

And, in dead center of Argon, is Opus. The single jutting set of cliffs is well-portrayed, and every detail is covered. It's as if I were looking down on it. Beautiful. But the rattlesnake designs at the edges of the map disturb me. What do they mean?

"As you can see," Byhi says, interrupting my thoughts, "This is a map of Argon. All of this will be the Pauraque's, and I shall govern it wisely." Byhi fingers the edging, and I cannot take my eyes away from the rattlesnakes. Their eyes sear and lock onto mine, their fangs almost glistening as if in the moonlight. The top two are in the coiled position, but the bottom two snakes are stretched out, looking up and hissing at the map of Argon.

Byhi catches my gaze. "The rattlesnakes are the crest of the Pauraque. They shall strike fear and respect in the hearts of all owls." I nod. It makes sense. Usually snakes can make a great snack, but vipers aren't on the dinner menu. Every owl looks out for them for fear of being bitten on the fly-thru grab-and-go meal.

"Now," Byhi continues, "We have a few challenges in conquering Argon."

"Excuse me," I interrupt, "Am I hearing this right? We're going to conquer all of Argon?" Byhi stares at me as if I had a missing beak.

"The Pauraque is more powerful than any-bird ever realized. It is possible, and we will pull it off. Nothing is beyond the reach of the Pauraque."

I nod again, a silent apology. Byhi huffs in approval, accepting my apology, then continues.

"I'd say that we have three main obstacles and one inner problem. The first obstacle is getting the masses. We need support from the entire population, which includes a large amount in Arko Forest and the Bleian Desert.

"The second thing is Worte Marsh. We don't know what to do with it. There is no evidence of owl residence whatsoever, and most of the search parties we've sent in haven't reported back." Byhi seems slightly nervous, something very uncharacteristic of her, and looks to the Pauraque.

"Well, we'll have to fix that then." The Pauraque remarks. She shifts on her perch, and with the uneasy silence, Byhi presses on.

"The third problem is the Snowy owls. There are a few of them left in the Dilecta Arctic, and they could pose serious threat to our operation. I suggest that we take them down sometime in our march. They will be a high priority.

"Finally, we have the internal problem. Arne."

The Pauaraque takes the prompt. "Arne shall be dealt with." She assures Byhi, "But I need you to keep her here. No more tastes of freedom, and cut her rations. We have to break her." I can barely make out the Pauraque turning towards me.

"I warn you now. She either rises to the occasion and gains a high position, or remains a prisoner and a slave the rest of her life."

"Yes, Pauraque," I acknowledge humbly. I can see the glint of the Pauraque's eyes as she blinks and turns back to the map. Intyl has stayed silent the whole time, and now Byhi turns to him.

"Celfina said that you claimed you could find information from anyone, from anyplace, by any means." Byhi searches Intyl, who tries to shrink away and avert his eyes. "It is time to earn your rank." Byhi points towards the word "Hunting Grounds" in Arko Forest. "Find out what connections we have there."

"Any additional guidelines?" Intyl asks respectfully. Byhi ponders for a moment, then turns to Intyl.

"Yes. If they try to stop you then…" Byhi flicks a claw, as if the detail was unimportant.

"…kill them."

Ayia

I am interested in the organization that has Tyrn worried. If something makes him worried then all of us have a right to worry about it. A lot.

I can have a reputation of being skeptical. I'm always the owl in the crowd that asks the questions that pertain to what we currently know; I always keep reality in my sight line and am never the first to believe conspiracy theories. This matter is especially hard to believe, but if Tyrn is already inclined to believe these owls, then maybe I should be more open.

The Burrow is downwind, and the blizzard carries us quickly to our destination. We twenty snowies soar on outstretched wings, all eyes focused on the Burrow. Tyrn and I land first, starting down the ramp and further into the Burrow. Tyrn quickly disappears, and I continue down, eager to see the owls.

As I round the corner, I expect to see some large owls. Perhaps some Great greys or even a Great Horned owl. But it was a rag-tag band of beat up owlets. A scratched Barn owl stares up at me, noticing Tyrn's return and how he brought friends. A Saw-whet owl and a couple of Burrowing owls hang back, watching me. They aren't afraid though. It appears that they've seen my kind before.

I continue to walk deeper into the chamber, and other snowies shuffle in. Soon we're all looking at them, and they're looking at us in awe.

Tyrn prompts the older Burrowing owl. "I have assembled them, as promised."

"We are the Snowy Ghosts," I introduce, continuing to watch the group of owls. They hold my gaze, staring back, unwavering.

"I am Nara," the older Burrowing owl says, "This is my sister Cici, and my friends Kari and Rhi. We have come to seek your help against a threat to all owls. And most importantly, these birds have proclaimed their power by capturing Arne." The crowd stays silent, preferring to let Nara speak.

But it switches to Rhi. "I have experienced first-hand of their cruelty. I was a slave to them once, and have seen their organization grow under the rule of a bird called the Pauraque. She desires to enslave all birds, and has her sights set on you snowies.

"When I first met Arne, she was defiant in the face of the authority I had cowered under for so many years. She led me to safety, and in the ensuing battle, drew them away so that we'd have a chance to go get help.

"You see, you're all we have. You're the last chance for saving Argon."

"Wait," I interrupt, "Are you implying that the Pauraque wishes to take over all of Argon? But this has never been done before, and it will not ever be done."

Rhi looks me straight in the eye. "If they can reign in Arne, what do you think they can do on a large scale?"

"Kari, Cici and I have known Arne personally," Nara explains, "She was the first to be attacked by a Eurasian eagle owl called Byhi. We banded together, and after some more encounters with the Pauraque's soldiers, they finally captured her.

"What she's doing now is anyone's guess. But if we're going to bring the Pauraque down then Arne's depending on you. We now have an owl on the inside, but it will mean nothing without your power to execute it."

"You do realize what a big decision this is? Not only do we have to believe you in the first place, but we have to willingly give our lives to help. I'm sure you're aware that by nature we are solitary predators and do not care about your matters." I inform them. The little Burrowing owl that must be Cici comes up to me with fire in her eyes, daring me to take it a step further.

"My friend Theo gave his life to try and help Arne," Cici growls, emotion almost cracking her voice in both anger and sadness, "Don't you realize! If we don't stop this, if we don't seize our chance to take them by surprise, you're next! This isn't a matter that doesn't concern you! This is a threat to your freedom and your very lives! We need to stand and *end* this."

"Bold words spoken by a little owl," I remark.

"I said the same thing, but she tells the truth. She is not lying about the Pauraque, and if she's set her sights on all of Argon, only the Two Owls could have a chance of stopping her unless we do this *now*." Tyrn chuckles, his voice going from laughter to a point with an edge.

"I'll see what I can do. I need time and proof though. I don't just give my help out to anyone. Owls, I haven't helped anyone in my life." I say. I turn to go, then pause. "Ayia." I introduce, as if sealing a deal. Then I'm out of the Burrow, launching myself into the frigid air, breathing deeply.

If what they say is true, then my homeland will be free no more.

Arne

Now I always have a cocky smile on my face, and the soldiers are starting to notice. They've let me see too much of their operation, and now I know what's going on. And not all of it is good for them.

The biggest thing I've found out is that some owls are looking for a more *honorable* leader, and Byhi hasn't quite delivered yet. I can use this to my advantage. Everyone wants a strong, famous owl to lead them, and right now Byhi is a no-name. If I can revert the attention to me, then maybe a rebellion will start from the inside.

And then it hits me...is my group really trying to get me out? It was my own flaw that killed Theo, that blasted claw that had been damaged by the stupid thorn. It hadn't been strong enough to hold him. So am I still in the group?

Let's just say they still like me. They could just walk away and continue on with their lives. Who wants to risk their lives to save another owl?

Cici did, a voice in my head reminds me, *she saved you. And then you saved her and allowed yourself to get captured. And then you did it again this last rescue mission; you drew them away and sacrificed yourself.*

But do I really care that much? Is that why I did it? Well...one great mystery at a time. And first I need to get out of here.

So...let's just say they're planning yet another rescue mission. Let's just say. If they attack from the outside, and I get the captured owls to attack from the inside, then the Pauraque's organization is sure to fall. It will be attacked on both fronts. Brilliant. But now...would they really come to save me?

None of the soldiers want to mess with me, and I'm being neglected. Food comes less often. So my intimidation has its pros and cons. But my wing is finally healing fully. It won't be long before I will yet again feel like I'm in my prime. I will once again be able to take on Byhi or any other owl that dares challenge me.

Tonight the moon is full and, surprisingly, my strength is great despite the conditions. I shoot up through the roof and taste the night air, almost sighing. I land perfectly on the edge, no longer feeling the chains on my feet. Nothing can hold me here. I am in my element. The night's shroud coats my feathers with mist and shadows, and I glow otherworldly, my purely white feathers looking as if they were made of moonlight-kissed snow.

I draw to my full height, and point my beak at the sky. I rip off a loud screech, my chorus of followers joining in answer. I hear a couple skirmishes farther off, where soldiers try and silence us. But we will not be stopped. We will be heard. And our numbers are growing.

We're like wolves howling at the moon. We howl and howl and won't cease. I know Byhi's listening. Let her hear. Let her hear the cries of the owls who know the truth, and who will fight for a rightful and, more importantly, *truthful*, leader.

Really, we say that they shouldn't have a leader at all. We should be free! We will earn our freedom, whether she likes it or not. Our wings should not be bound. We must fly. We *will* fly, away from here and back to where we belong.

They are bold words spoken by prisoners, implied in our nightly screeches. But we cannot be stifled. And I will make sure of that.

When we are satisfied, we give a final booming hoot, and fly back down to my cell. I hit the dirt floor, and all of a sudden I feel light-headed, but I don't care. My stomach growls, but I don't care. I now care about leading these owls to safety if they know of Byhi's lies. If they have resisted, then I will help them escape.

"Arne?" a voice asks. I turn towards the door, vision slightly blurred, and see Nyk. I growl deep in my throat. It's answer enough.

Nyk looks at the ground for a moment, and then looks back up at me. "I just wanted to inform you that there will be a Recruitment. You can either come with me or I'll leave you to the soldier escorts."

I snort, but he persists. "I'll be less rough," he promises. I snort again, but sigh in defeat. He smiles a little, and walks over to me, unhooking my chains from the wall and leading me through the metal-reinforced wooden door down the dirt passageway, those same flickering torches almost winking at me as I pass by. They waver as we pass, their delicate orange flowers bending in the slightest gale.

Nyk walks in silence. He seems partially regretful. He better be. He joined the Pauraque. He's helping the same birds who captured him in the first place. Where's the logic in that?

Looking at him makes me doubt my plan. It makes more tears form in my eyes, and I have to fight them back. Have these owls really resisted? If Nyk can't, then what owl can?

Me, a voice inside me says. I *will be the one to finally resist.*

***

I'm pretty sure I can call her my archenemy. Maybe nemesis would fit her better. She's vile to me either way.

Lady Byhi. She perches proud and tall on the rocky ledge, right where Celfina used to be. I sort of understand it now. They all come and go. Everyone's replaceable. Even Byhi. I'm sure the Pauraque knows that, she's just letting Byhi think she's important. Byhi could've been better off wearing a sign that says "*I'm a puppet*".

The Twin Wings cover her left and right flanks. They seem to care about the individuality of an owl, but they aren't much better. They recruit. They force owls to serve in this organization. No one here holding rank is clean-clawed.

"I'm sure everyone knows how the Recruitment goes," Byhi says, addressing the crowd of frightened and over-worked owls. A sea of nervous bobbing heads ripples before Byhi.

"Good," she coos, "I trust you will follow the usual procedures."

The Twin Wings step forward, their white feathers ruffling in the slight breeze, their ethereal eyes glowing like jade. Nope, nothing weird about those twin barn owls at all.

"Our top pick is a well-known owl here," They proclaim, "Arne, you have been chosen." I growl, and all the owls around me immediately look at me, slightly nervous but also anxious to see what happens.

"Come, perch beside me." Pyre beckons. I give a short, sharp screech in reply, and Pyre gazes at me angrily, completely in control but also starting to become annoyed. "I am done with your rebellion. Accept my offer or be claimed by Ruole."

"I belong to no one," I boom, "And will be claimed by no owl. Think what you want but my talons are planted right here." The crowd of owls looks back at the Twin Wings for their response, grim slashes of defiance set on each owl's features. Whispers of agreement about my actions circulate around me, fading in and out like wisps in the wind.

"This is all a game to you, isn't it?" I venture, targeting Byhi, "We are your little pawns, controlled by the almighty queen." I look at Byhi, and see a flicker of doubt behind her eyes. "But...you aren't the queen, are you?"

"I have always been the queen! Now the Pauraque will help me show every single owl that very fact!" Byhi shouts, angered at my deduction.

"Byhi, you're the player," I continue, "The masquerade. You appear to be in control, so that if something goes wrong, you'll be the one to fall. The Pauraque set it all up perfectly. If this plan fails, if I beat you, you die and the Pauraque walks away unscathed, ready to start the next game."

"No! You are wrong! I will be forevermore! I am LADY BYHI!" Byhi screeches. "Show her!" she commands the Twin Wings.

The Twin Wings' eyes flicker to blood red, rage filling them to the brim. I had put together the plans of the Pauraque and told them to the whole crowd. In an instant the Twin Wings no longer stay the wise controllers; they become the slave-masters. They know when to crack down the whip.

They lock eyes onto mine and let their claws fall off the edge, soaring through the air. The crowd parts, giving them a patch of earth to land on in front of me. Their feathers stand on end, and both Pyre and Ruole walk towards me, anger radiating from them like a heat source.

"You will fall like every other owl before you," they threaten, their voices layered over one another's in perfect unison. The owls on the front lines edge away, their fear showing in their wide eyes.

"I doubt that," I growl. Like a timed routine the Twin Wings raise launch themselves into the air, using their talons to lunge for me. In reaction I dodge and roll underneath them, and once I'm clear of their feet I travel backwards, hurling them onto the ground, their beaks smashing into the dirt. Of course, they quickly get back up, and like twin tornadoes, go to work at trying to defeat me in sparring.

I screech boldly and plunge into the flurry of claws and white feathers. We must look like a violent blizzard, impossible to tell one body from another. We twirl and parry, jab and aim careful blows. Together, they manage to punch me in the beak, and I go end over end. But I land on my feet, and reverse my momentum, crashing back into them. I forget about everyone around me, and focus on the battle at hand. If I win this I give hope back to everyone who's watching. My rebel group will see this as a cue to get ready for the end game.

I get a surge of strength, a final push. It's unfamiliar but invigorating, so with my undamaged wing I ram the Twin Wings and send them flying across the room. I stumble slightly but manage to stop my momentum and put on the brakes, watching as the Twin Wings sail through the air, defeated even though they had the advantage in numbers.

I turn to Byhi. "You've always been outnumbered, you just didn't know it."

"Can't you add?" Byhi shrieks, dumbly falling into my trap, "It was two to one!"

"All the more reason that you should be scared," I retort, making my point. Byhi growls in frustration, and she lets it escape from her throat into a screech.

"You know that you've been beaten by a single owl," I yell. "You try and mold me into your perfect secret weapon. Well, this clay has hardened, and can no longer be shaped."

"It will be cracked and shattered then if I cannot mold it!" Byhi screeches, ignorant to the fact that I have her right where I want her, and she's losing control in her own element.

"Clay, once dried, is very tough. You cannot simply throw a couple hammers at it and expect it to give." I reply. The Twin Wings shake off some dirt, and look up at me, scowling, realizing I was referring to *them*.

"They aren't hammers," Byhi growls, glaring at the Twin Wings, "But they are sticks who wish they were made of metal."

"Why did you really call us here?" I ask, getting down to business. Byhi smiles, admiring how I figured out that the Recruitment wasn't the main focus.

"I called all of you here to give Arne an invaluable piece of information that could help her prepare in time," Byhi says. She focuses on me, her gaze hungry like the promise of a stack of gold bars. "Soon, we shall see what you are made of. I will gather everyone to see the great Arne fall under the crushing weight of the skill of my armies. Even Arne has her limits. So I want to press them."

A few deluded owls hoot, "For the Pauraque! For Lady Byhi! Lady Byhi!" and their hoots grow in number, but amid the crowd, a few owls turn their heads towards me, silent. I nod, and we all raise our heads to the ceiling. We screech simultaneously, drowning out any other sound. The might of our cries shocks all the birds into silence, and Byhi stares in amazement. She starts to try and pick out the traitors, but many other owls in the crowd realize that if they don't pipe up then the rebels will be ratted out, and so they join in the screech. Soon over half the crowd has lifted their cries to the full moon, and as our song dies away, Byhi grows hopping mad.

"We will not cheer your name!" I shout, standing tall for all the owls that are watching. "I represent all the owls here that have seen through your lies, and I dare say that your time here is short. We do not support you. We will not stand for you!" Byhi literally shakes in anger.

"Leave my sight!" she screams. She looks at our motionless figures. "All of you!" she shrieks. The Twin Wings screech once and all of them scramble, filing into lines out of the rocky center, myself among the sea of feathers.

As I enter the passageway, the Twin Wings hone in and pluck me from the throng of owls. They guide me back to my cell, and linger for a moment before closing the door. Their white frames glow in the lower lighting.

"Do you know the reason..." Pyre begins.

"...why you won?" Ruole asks. I don't answer, and they take it as an invitation for their explanation. "A third omniscient was involved," Ruole says, sad for herself.

I pause in surprise. "A what?"

"A third party omniscient was involved," Pyre repeats.

"We are of the Fate Owl," they announce in unison.

"So you..." Ruole says.

"Must be with the Destiny Owl," Pyre concludes. I blink a few times, trying to process the meaning in their words. But then they are gone, the metal-barred wooden door had been closed with barely a sound.

The Destiny Owl? I know Kari was obsessed with which side she was on, but I had never given much thought. The Dilecta Arctic hardly heard anything of that sort. But now that the Twin Wings mention the words, they send shivers down my spine. What they said was true. It wasn't me who had the strength. The Twin Wings had some help too, and they were quite possibly undefeatable with the Fate Owl. But apparently I'd tapped into the Destiny Owl and it had saved my hide. Lucky me.

But there truly is a lot of planning to do. Byhi is setting up my execution. And I know the number of owls I've fought before were only small bands. I can't imagine whole armies. The meetings she holds like the one today, they show only a fraction of the workers that make the operation run. But their warriors...

Nyk. Will he be the one leading them into battle, setting up my death? Has he really slipped that far? All I know is that I will turn my death into the freedom of others. That will be where our rebel group will make our final stand.

Cici

I don't get how long it takes for them to choose whether to help us or not. The answer should be "yes, I will kill all the birds that were involved in kidnapping Arne and killing Theo". But no, they want to hold a meeting and discuss it like some high-rolling owls. They don't get the severity of the situation, and how crucial it is to stop the Pauraque from taking over Argon.

Ayia leaves. Tyrn seems like he understands our urgency, and is trying to rally the snowies, but the enthusiasm isn't there with the others.

"Maybe you won't believe us till you experience it for yourselves," I mumble. Nara does a double-take at me, and then leans forward.

"That's a great idea!" she whispers. She stands, leaning heavily on her good leg, and all eyes rest on her.

"If you cannot decide, we must show you proof. You have to come with us and see the Pauraque at Opus." Nara declares. Tyrn hesitates in answer.

"You cannot be serious," some-bird whines from the crowd, "We are on the other side of the arctic. We will not make such a journey on the whim and stories of some owlets."

Tyrn stands tall, looking the speaker in the eye. "Look at them, up and down. How much do you think they've been through? Look at Nara." Nara blushes slightly, but the wounds on her leg is all too obvious. Tyrn gestures toward Rhi as well. "Observe the scratches on Rhi. Do you see how wide they are? The wider the slashes, the bigger the claws, the bigger the bird. You don't think they ran into something like a Great horned owl by chance, do you? Are their wounds all from bumping into some owl as they flew by?"

Mumbles echo through the assembly. I grow impatient, and wonder what Nara is planning. Nara clears her throat quietly, and continues.

"Opus has become their main base of operations. If you'll pay them a visit, you'll see it for yourself. We'll escort you there." But the crowd's attention is wandering.

"Hey!" I yell. Murmurs grow in volume, and they ignore me. I screech loudly, surprising everyone. It booms in the Burrow, and shakes the walls. "Do I have your attention now?" I ask, annoyed. Grumbles erupt in the crowd, but I see some nods.

"Look, I know that you don't want to leave the comfort of your icy perches, but this is a serious matter. I'll fight you right here, right now if I have to if it makes you see that I'm not backing down until you help us. Yeah, you might be a little taken aback, and before I met Arne I would've never said anything this offensive. But I am. Because I'm no owlet. None of us are inexperienced or naive, and none of us aren't warriors now, either. Now, we are your advantages in taking down these owl-pellet birds. If you are going to help, then you're going to need what we've learned to beat them." Of course, there were a couple smiles at my bad language, but it made my point. Then Ayia marches in, ready to speak her mind.

"We can't just march all the way to Opus without being spotted," Ayia says, back from her trip, "If you haven't noticed, our feathers are completely white."

"Arne strolled right in there," I point out, "Apparently they hadn't set up sentries or guards right outside of Opus. They were more tightly clustered at the actual cliffs." Ayia isn't buying it.

"So, we just fly over there and say hi? Then fly right back?" Ayia asks. I scowl at her.

"Oh yeah, we're just going to take a little stroll. No, we're going to have to be ready. Just going is a commitment for all of you. But that didn't stop us from getting here. We're desert owls, and forest owls! We're not built for the Dilecta Arctic. Why else would we travel here unless it was matters of our very lives? That is, unless we were crazy owls. But has our logic not given points that would rule out the possibility of insanity?" I say.

"This *is* insanity," Ayia sighs.

"Then you are admitting that the threat is real!" I protest. Ayia growls a complaint, but no one takes notice.

I'm so frustrated and fed up with these owls! Can't they see how important it is to stop the Pauraque?

I turn to leave. "Are you coming or not?" I growl. The sea of Snowy owls look from one owl to the other, but no one dares take a step forward. No one wants to promise anything.

"Alright," Nara mutters, following me out the door. Kari hovers beside Nara, quietly giving her support as Nara limps out of the Burrow. I glance back and see Rhi lagging behind.

Rhi opens her beak to say something, then decides against it, and continues walking, turning her back on the audience. Tyrn looks as if he wants to say goodbye or maybe join us, but we've cleared the Burrow. The snow is still flying, and it stings my face through my feathers. But we take off anyway. We don't have anything left to do here, so we should head back to Opus.

"What are we going to do?" Kari asks, bringing up an important matter, "Certainly our band is not enough to pose much of a threat. That's why we came here in the first place, right?"

"I don't know," I sigh, "All I know is that those snowies aren't going to listen to us. We can't convince them."

Nara nods in agreement. "There isn't anything we could say that wouldn't change their minds."

"Not even the existence of an owl scarred by slavery," Rhi mutters to herself. We all fall silent at that, turning our attention to focusing on keeping steady in the whipping gale. I can't see the horizon ahead, and wonder which way we flew in to get here. We might become lost in this blizzard.

Nyk

I perch on the ledge, looking out over Argon. The Pauraque plans to conquer all of it, to enslave every single owl. How can I go through with this? I know I'm on the inside because I'm doing this to save Arne. But I can't just stand back and watch my world fall to the claws of the Pauraque. I do all of this for Arne. And I keep that in mind to not loose myself in my fake world.

"Nyk," some-owl whispers behind me. Her voice is full of longing. I turn around, and see Byhi, her eyes fixed on me from beneath her silver mask. "Intyl was going to leave for the mission, but the Pauraque has gone against my judgment." She steps closer, and my mind races. What has the Pauraque decided?

"She wants you to go in Intyl's place," she whispers. I am stunned, but I manage to keep a straight face. Me. I will go out to help make Argon fall. To destroy my own homeland, and kill innocent owls.

I turn away from Byhi, and search the dry ground, trying to keep it together. They think I'm just as evil as them. I cannot show emotion.

Byhi senses my hesitation, and steps even closer. "You don't have to go," she offers, "I will tell the Pauraque you are on your way, and send Intyl instead." Byhi looks me in the eye, worry slightly lining her features. "You can stay with me," she whispers.

Her eyes sparkle slightly, and although the fire of her power is still going, longing of a partner to share it with is visible. And for a split second, I see a lovely owl, some-bird who was alone and only wanted company when her dreams come true. But a small voice whispers in my head, and her face morph's into Arne's. I have to stay on target. I make one wrong move and Arne dies.

"I'm sorry," I say, abruptly ending the moment. Byhi's longing turns to sadness as she desperately tries to hold onto me.

"Wait!" she calls, but I fly to the launch platform. The gray wooden platform hovers like a balcony, and I perch on it, preparing to carry out the Pauraque's new orders. Byhi persists, and flies onto the launch pad, her mood turning into anger.

"It's Arne, isn't it," she says bitterly. I cannot meet Byhi's irate gaze, otherwise it will give it away. Byhi sees this and grows irate and impatient.

"Go then," she commands coldly. I silently depart and follow orders, leaving Byhi behind. I keep my gaze on the horizon and my thoughts on Arne.

I will not let you down, Arne.

***

The forest only has one commonality with the arctic. And that's getting slapped in the face with leaves where normally, in the arctic, you'd get slapped in the face with snow. I bet you'd get slapped in the face with sand in the desert, and you'd get slapped in the face with vines in the marsh. How can I avoid being slapped in the face?

Staying at Opus? Wrong! Arne would slap me in the face too!

And Arko Forest is much too hot and humid. As much as I hate it, I can't even imagine Worte Marsh; it must be ten times more humid with loads more bugs. And, worst of all, I'm not looking forward to completing the reason why I'm enduring all of this.

I have to capture other owls for the Pauraque.

This goes against the whole plan that I set in motion. I am trying to help Arne escape by working within the higher ranks. I didn't think that I would have to carry on Byhi's plans in order to keep my cover. Quite a fatal mistake, huh?

I break into a clearing, and see the masks of the soldiers that fell here. I remember the stories, and look around. Sure enough, there's a hollow spot in one of the trees. *This is where Arne was first encountered the Pauraque's soldiers,* I recall.

I stop in mid-flight. *Why haven't I thought of it before? I could just run right now!*

No...it's too easy. Byhi wouldn't have sent me on my first mission without someone watching me. I have to be careful and look for clues as to if any-bird is following me. If I intend to free Arne, then I'm going to have to keep making Byhi, Intyl, and the Pauraque believe that I'm still on their side, and that I've changed into one more of their puppets. That I'm completely loyal.

I pause to listen to my surroundings. Nothing. No rustles in the bushes or wing-beats in the distance. The only sounds are the far-off calls of the local birds, carrying on with their daily chatter and gossip. They will have no idea what hit them. And if things go as the

Pauraque wants no one will be left to say that they were even hit at all.

Kari

I didn't think it could get any colder. I am wrong. It gets *much* colder once you've been sheltered from it and have to go back out again. The warmth I regained from spending some time in the Burrow is instantly lost once we start flying.

The real problem is that my wings are still damp. The fall down into the snow had dampened my feathers, and they didn't have enough time to dry back at the Burrow. So, my damp wings are going to freeze here. And I'm going to die!

I can feel the temperature of the feathers coating my wings start to drop. If I don't get out of this weather, they'll freeze over, and I won't be able to fly.

"Stay together!" Rhi shouts, and we try and keep formation. Cici and Nara stick together, flying side by side. Rhi leads us out; probably because she remembers the way we came, and is thus the only one who won't get us lost. I bring up the rear, struggling not to let the wind flip me over in flight.

We try and cover some ground, but soon Nara and I fall behind. I can tell Nara's leg is bothering her. And with one look, Nara realizes what's wrong with my wings.

"When you fell...I thought you looked a little bedraggled." She says loudly, trying to be heard above the wind.

"I can't be up here much longer," I tell her, the wind threatening me, trying to make me go capsize.

"I can't either, my leg is going to freeze," Nara agrees, nodding her head. I look out to where Cici and Rhi are, black shapes in the blizzard. They don't stop flying.

"Rhi! Cici!" I yell, but my words are taken by the wind. "Wait here!" I order Nara, and she obliges, as that was the only thing she could do.

"Rhi! Cici!" I shout, using every vocal cord I had. I screech at the top of my lungs, but the shapes of my friends are fading. I struggle against the wind, trying to catch up with them, pushing myself. But my wings are growing stiff, and the cold sickness is spreading throughout me. I try to call them back one last time, but it's no use. They're gone.

I look back, but Nara is gone too. "Nara!" I scream, now letting the wind take me back. But Nara isn't there. I know she was right here. Right here. But she's gone. It's impossible to pinpoint where we really were in this world of white.

They're all gone. Nara could die here in the cold. *I* could die here. Maybe Rhi and Cici will have a better chance. If they have to stop and rest, they'll have each other's warmth to survive on, and they're not injured as badly as we are, so it's likely that they'll keep going.

But how long till they realize that they lost us? Then they'll turn around and look for us. But they won't find us, I can feel it. Then they'll die in the storm too.

I'm amazed at how I'm already thinking of how to save Rhi and Cici from dying when I'm not quite down yet either. But it's only a matter of time. I have maybe minutes left before I'm frozen, literally.

I have a hard time hovering, but I manage. I have to sort this out. It was so fast; it was just boom and they're gone.

But I didn't even have minutes. I go to flap my wings, and they won't move. I drop like a stone to the icy ground below.

Chapter 9: Rebellion

Narrator

Byhi flits around, picking and rearranging things to make it perfect. A gnarled branch rises from the middle of a pile of things, gray and twisted. Byhi picked it out herself. She entwines little rocks in the branch for decoration as well.

The ground from which it rises has four little sections. In one pile is a patch of dirt with some vibrant green weeds in it. Right next to it is a pile of golden sand with some dead twigs, and in back of the branch is another patch of dirt, with puddles of water and thick weeds growing in the dirt. And to the back left is some white sand, a clear rock sitting off-center in it. Of course, Byhi means for it to represent the country of Argon. The Arko Forest is the patch of dirt with all the little green weeds, and the Bleian Desert is the pile of golden sand with the dead twigs in it. The Worte Marsh is the wetter clump of dirt that has more dense weeds. And then, in the back, is the white sand as the Dilecta Arctic, the clear rock being the Glacier. And smack in the middle of all of it is the gnarled branch that has pebbles entwined in it, serving as both a perch and a representation of Opus, the jutting center of cliffs that separates the four ecosystems.

Byhi steps back from her work, pleased with herself. This will make a perfect command center. All owls will answer to her here, and when they bow their heads they will look at what is beneath her perch and be reminded of how she rules over all of Argon. That is, once she conquers it. But it cannot be that hard. She has planned it all out, and no threat can stop her.

True, the snowy owls in the arctic unnerves her, but she can take care of them. Nothing will stand in her way. What owl can stop her?

No. Arne. She is the only threat. The thought hits Byhi like a freight train. Arne has to be eliminated or Byhi's plans still have that zero-point-zero-zero-one percent chance of failing.

Byhi's expression grows darker as her thoughts turn to owlicide. She has to get rid of Arne before she can be care-free. Byhi doesn't care what the Pauraque thinks. Arne must be taken care of. Arne is the only one standing in-between her and Nyk.

"Lady Byhi," a voice says behind her. Byhi turns around wildly, but becomes embarrassed of her panic because it was only Intyl. He is bowing respectfully, quivering ever so slightly.

"What Intyl?" Byhi groans, "Can't you see I'm busy here?"

"The Pauraque wishes to speak with you," Intyl says.

Byhi knew that the words "the Pauraque wishes to speak with you" means "the Pauraque commands that you go to her chambers so she can give orders". But the way Intyl says it...the reason sounds important.

"Tell the Pauraque I'll be right there," Byhi sighs. Intyl bows once more, and then scurries off to carry the reply.

Byhi growls in frustration. The Pauraque can do a lot of things, but she better not read minds; otherwise she'll ban Byhi from carrying out her plans.

***

"I've called you on a certain matter concerning Arne," the Pauraque says, smoothly beginning the conversation. Byhi winces. Maybe the Pauraque *can* read minds. "I know you feel my judgment might be faulty on keeping Arne alive, but I assure you, Intyl and Nyk will turn her around. She will be a tool at our disposal."

"Yes, Pauraque," Byhi quickly agrees, "I did not mean for you to think that I would doubt your decisions." Byhi silently fumes. *Nyk and Intyl will turn her around. Hmph. Nyk certainly* is *turning towards her.*

"Yet you were planning to dispose of Arne," the Pauraque persists. Byhi can feel the sweat rising through her feathers.

"Never lie to me," the Pauraque orders, her poisonous brown eyes glinting in the shadows, "And tell me your every intention. No secrets. I will then clarify what should be done. And do not be afraid to tell me, because if you don't, I *will* find out."

Byhi nods, now not just nervous but solemn as well. She cannot even keep her own thoughts from the Pauraque now.

***

"Being Lady Byhi is hard," Byhi complains to one of her servant owls. The servant owl looks up at her and nods in respect, hoping that some sympathy was shown on her face. Byhi accepts the gesture and goes back to staring out over Argon. "I mean, you have to deal with management, which owls will join the army, and which owls have really good talon-sharpening skills, like you, for example." Byhi rattles on. The servant owl keeps nodding at appropriate times, continuing her work.

"And Intyl, he's a little weak. I trust that the Twin Wings do their job, but Celfina didn't know a thing. She was a twisted feather in my wing. And Rikki, he was pushy. He should've never treated me the way he did when he first brought me to the Paurauqe. Nasty little bird. I'm glad they're both gone.

"Nyk isn't bad. He's a pretty, and seems loyal. He'll bring back some nice owls that will work hard. He'll do anything for me. But one thing he won't do is leave Arne for me. He's too attached. I must get rid of Arne."

"You are Lady Byhi," the servant says politely, "You can do anything. Even if it is taming a snowie."

"Yes," Byhi purrs, "I am able to do the impossible."

Arne

I test my chains every day. They are solid and supposedly unbreakable, but I broke the last manacle. But with two shackles, it is double the resistance. It takes a lot more effort, and compared to last time, I don't know how much more effort I have to give.

Then again, now I am of full health. And my training has stopped for some reason, so I constantly have excess energy. True, my rations have been cut, but from all the years of living in the unforgivable arctic, I learn to adapt. It does not hinder me in the slightest.

So I have continued screeching at night, the number of my followers growing. I have nicknamed us, "The Callers", because we call out into the night for other owls to see where they are and what has truly happened. More and more owls join with every chorus, and now I wonder if the whole population in Opus is lifting their voices to the dark skies above, but then the next night more join in, and the noise grows considerably louder, and it reaches farther into Opus. Tonight, if we try hard enough, I believe we can reach outside of Opus and farther into Argon.

The night is young, and I continue scratching on the dirt floor. All the Callers do it now. I scratch a circle with intricate designs directly under the opening in the ceiling. Once the moon is directly above and its beams line up with the drawing, I'll fly up and start the Call. One night I had mentioned this to a nearby owl, and she had passed it on, the next one passing it on to his neighbor owl, and so on. Now we screech simultaneously.

I beat my wings with grace, rising through the vertical-tunnel ceiling and past its open top, launching myself into the frigid night air. The cold feels good on my feathers and it lets my senses unfold like a flower, blossoming so that I'm totally in-tune with my surroundings.

I don't know why the Pauraque built this design, what her intent was, but now it is the tool of rebellion. I blink once, looking up at the moon. It emanates soft wisps of silver, and it floats down from the unreachable parts of the skies, settling onto my feathers like stardust. It's just beautiful, tonight. I wish it would be like this forever, but it is wishful thinking in the first place. I have to lead these owls to freedom, and my full attention is going to be needed when the time comes.

I wait the two second count as tradition calls, and then I screech to the stars above. The signal goes, and like a wave, owls from all around Opus join in the Call. We use every ounce of air in our lungs, and we try and give every feeling of power, of hope, of strength into the screech. I know the Pauraque is listening. And I know she gets the message...

...we know what is going on, and you will fall.

But tonight, something is different. A low rumbling washes over us, creeping over every stone; it vibrates everything in its path. After a few seconds of listening, I know what it is.

Byhi is hooting, trying to break the sounds of our rebellion. I can hear her trying to urge her soldiers to join her, to try and stop our Call. Slowly, some of the ranks join in, and it makes me shiver. The low rumble creeps into my ears like ivy, as if it is some dark energy. Like chanting.

I take a quick breath and screech louder, with everything I have. My followers can hear the lead and push their screeches, our Call now resounding not only all around and within Opus, but into the lands in the distance, to the forest, desert, marsh, and arctic. I hope Nara and Cici and Kari can hear. I hope they're still alive.

Byhi's side of hoots grows in number, their sounds of repressing force and fear corrupting the night. But as Byhi urges the soldiers to push harder, I can hear some of the ranks breaking into screech, joining the Call. In a matter of seconds both Byhi's army and Byhi's workers are screeching their heads off, defying their authority and joining the Call.

After a time, we die away, retiring. But smiles must be on all of our faces. Because we've won tonight. And Byhi knows it.

I jump down the hole and glide back to my spot, landing without a sound. I feel invigorated, but I know it won't last for long. There will be consequences for my actions. Byhi will find out who led this attack, and she will try and kill them. But it will be me. And so far the Pauraque wants me alive.

I am untouchable, or at least for now. As long as the Pauraque believes she can turn me into one of her perfect little soldiers, I'm going to be allowed to live. But what she doesn't know is that I'll never turn. No one can make me fight with the very owls I'm trying to stop. Not like they did with Nyk.

Anger starts to boil up inside of me, and I press against my chains. They strain but pull taut, and some cracks are heard from the wall. I pause. These walls must be affected from the large temperature change, which makes them weaker. Sometimes winds from the Bleian Desert comes in and scorches everything, and sometimes the gale from the Dilecta Arctic blows in and puts a coat of frost on everything. It *must* affect the integrity of the walls greatly.

I test my chains once more. A few more nights. A few more nights and breaking the chains won't matter. The location of Opus itself will free me from my cell.

But I have to keep it secret. Any-bird finds out that the walls are crumbling around me and they'll move me to a new cell. I cannot test my chains again and show the cracks in the walls until the time is right.

Patience is the key...because the end game is nigh.

Nyk

"I know you're there," I growl. The bushes behind me rustle again, and I know I've found my follower.

"Come out slowly and I might not rip you apart," I snarl. I turn around, and see a quivering Eastern screech owl slowly come out from the foliage. Intyl looks up at me nervously, trying to crack a half-smile. "What are you doing here?" I ask him, "You're supposed to be back at Opus."

"Byhi sent me to watch you," Intyl explains.

"Of course," I sigh, "She doesn't trust me, does she?"

"No," Intyl says plainly.

"Well," I begin.

But Intyl interrupts. "I don't trust you either."

"Excuse me?"

Intyl looks me in the face. "I don't trust you either because you don't trust Byhi or the Pauraque. You never wanted to be a Bronze." His eyes fall a little, then he looks around to see if anyone is listening. He doesn't lift his gaze, but says "I don't trust them either."

"Well," I finish, "Then I'm your ally. We both don't like the position and situation we're in." Intyl nods.

"Have you heard the Call yet?" Intyl asks me.

"The what?"

"The Call. Don't tell Byhi obviously,"

"When would I ever report to Byhi truthfully?" I retort.

"Arne has started a rebellion," Intyl continues. I'm intrigued, and motion for him to continue. "At night, hundreds, maybe thousands of owls screech at the top of their lungs when the light of the moon reaches a circle they had drawn on the bottom of their cells. As story goes, Arne leads the choir, as a Call for every owl to see through Byhi's lies and join in the rebellion."

"There's already been a rebellion while I was gone?"

"In a way," Intyl clarifies, "Their screeching is full of hope in freedom and all that kind of stuff. The Pauraque hates it, and so does Byhi. Word went around that tonight they're going to try and drown out Arne with some Fate Owl Hoots."

As if out of a horror movie, the wind changes eerily just at the sound of it. "You know no owl is supposed to do that. It's dark energy; some owls say it can take away your ability to fly." I whisper nervously.

"Byhi's forcing the army to do it anyway!" Intyl hisses, "If Arne can't drown them out, then Byhi's entire worker population is going to die."

"Foolish," is the only word I could manage that could even vaguely describe what I thought of Byhi.

"That's why she needs you to bring in new owls. She'll 'cleanse' the old ones and then when the new ones come in she'll make sure that they won't rebel. It'll be a fresh start for Byhi." Intyl tells me.

I growl in frustration. Byhi. What a vile, evil, no-good, pellet-coughing…

"We need to head back and stop her," Intyl suggests. I turn to him. He's always been so quiet; I never thought I'd hear anything this rebellious come out of his beak.

"Yes," I agree, and we take flight, speeding back the way we came. The sun is setting, and the light is fading fast. "When exactly were they supposed to start the hoots?" I ask Intyl.

"Right after Arne starts the Call," Intyl answers, "Which would be just as the moon starts to climb into the sky."

"We're not going to make it," I mutter, but I fly harder anyway. The blood pounds in my ears as I try and warn Arne in time. But we're so far away from Opus, we won't get back till at least tomorrow, and that's if we fly all night long.

We're too late. A piercing cry of owls starts to split through the air, traveling far from its source. But soon the sound grows dark. A deep rhythmic hooting starts to rumble from Opus, trying to overtake the chorus of screeches.

But Arne leads them louder, pushing their limits. Soon the hooting dissolves into more screeches, and in a matter of minutes, the whole ordeal is over.

"One rebellious move at a time," Intyl mutters. We slow down our pace from break-neck to speedy, and continue flying to Opus.

What am I going to say when I come back empty-handed? *Hey, I didn't do what you wanted me to do because I hate you and how you like to enslave owls. I'm joining the rebels so free Arne right now or else.* Yeah, like Byhi's going to respond well to *that*.

Rhi

"Stay together!" I yell back to the rest of my group. I turn my attention back to looking ahead, trying to picture how we got here. I'm probably the only one here who remembers the way out, so I've got a lot of avian lives depending on me to lead them out of here. This white wasteland.

I despise snow. It's official. It seeps into my feathers, and makes me shiver uncontrollably. I think I remember that my parents didn't mind the cold so much, but I'm different. Snow and I don't mix.

In my complaining-rant I pick up speed, trying to get out of this blizzard as fast as possible. I hear Cici's wing-beats behind me, trying to keep up, but there is a lack of noise. Well, that isn't totally true, because the sound of the snow rushing by my ears tries to block everything else out, but...

I look back, and it's just as I feared. The only bird following me is Cici.

Cici sees my expression and looks back fearfully. No one else is there. They're gone. Kari and Nara aren't there.

Cici screams something. Her words are whipped away by the wind, but I can read her beak. *Nara!* But...they can't be gone. They just can't.

My brain won't compute what happened. I don't want to.

"Nara!" Cici screams again. Off to my left I barely make out an invisible shape that some snow is bending around...Ayia.

She appears out of nowhere. One second, there was snow, the next, she's hovering right here, between Cici and Cici screams for Nara and Kari one more time, and Ayia puts a claw on her shoulder.

"It's best you get under cover," she says, yelling above the wind.

"We can't!" Cici shouts, "We have to find Nara and Kari!"

Ayia seems slightly saddened, but it's gone quickly. "If you want to make it through the blizzard then come with me."

"No," Cici says. I look at Ayia.

"Maybe can you at least escort us out of here?" I plead. A flicker of surprise flits across the depths of her eyes, but she nods, accepting my request. She looks at the direction we were traveling, and heads towards the imaginary point, leading us through the storm.

***

It feels like forever, like I'm trudging through the snow. The air is thick with snowflakes, like I'm swimming through slush. But Ayia takes the brunt of it, shielding us from the worst of the blizzard. We dutifully fly behind her, keeping our heads down, just flying. Cici has frozen tears stuck on her feathers, and she seems bitter. I don't blame her though. She had to give up on her sister and leave her behind. She left behind any chances of her saving her sister back there.

"Are any other owls out here?" I ask. Ayia hesitates in her answer, but finally turns her head so I can hear her reply.

"Tyrn might have tried to follow me. If anyone can find your friends, it's Tyrn."

I'm not sure if Cici heard, but she smiles for a split second. It seems fake though. Like saying thank you when you really don't want to touch the present.

As we near the edge of the arctic, the blizzard starts to die away. It gets easier to fly, and the force of the winds starts to wane. Ayia slows down, and we see Arko Forest in the distance.

"This is your stop," Ayia says. She turns, hovering.

"That took forever," Cici mutters. Ayia rolls her eyes.

"That was the fastest I've ever traveled across the arctic. We were going with the wind, not against it."

"That was going *with* the wind?" I moan, "I feel like my wings are lead weights."

Ayia chuckles. "Well, good luck." Then she's gone again, her form melded into the world of white.

Cici looks at me, the wind ruffling her feathers. "How are we going to do this? We have no backup. You heard Kari. That's why we came in the first place; we needed more owls to fight with us, otherwise it wasn't going to work."

"We'll go anyway," I say, "I want to kick my master's tail-feathers for once."

"Well," Cici compensates, "How about we rest first? Please? I'm tired." I sigh. I'm exhausted as well.

"Okay," I mutter, "I guess the tail-feather-whooping stuff has to wait."

Kari

I wake up to flickering torches.

Tyrn perches beside me, his eyes closed. I groan, and sit up. My wings...they're dry. I look around the room, and realize that I'm in some kind of sheltered room; cold snow carpets the ground outside.

I flap my wings for a moment, lifting myself off the ground. My wings work fine now, as if nothing had happened.

Nara. She's still out there.

Tyrn wakes up, realizing that I'm awake. "Ah, you're okay then."

"What do you mean?" I ask.

"You've been out for a few days. You're wings were frozen over, maybe from some residual water from our first encounter. Chilled to the bone."

"But we have to find Nara..." I trail off. Tyrn seems regretful.

"We were snowed in. I went out a couple times before it got bad, but I didn't see anything." I shut my eyes tight. Just like that. Gone.

"I have to find Rhi and Cici then," I say, trying to put on a convincing determined-face. Tyrn gives one short laugh, but bobs his head in agreement.

"Alright, test out your wings," he orders gently. I comply; slowly beating my wings, then going faster and faster till I'm hovering a few inches off the ground. Tyrn frowns, inspecting them.

"I'm not sure how you'll be in the long-term, but you seem fine for now. If you feel like you can't hold straight, then just ask to stop. I don't want you falling from the sky." I release the breath I've been holding, and gently let myself down.

"So, we're off then?"

Tyrn nods, then shakes his head side to side as if he were weighing some possibilities. "It might take a day or so. And that's if we were flying as hard as we could."

"We will fly as fast as we can then," I growl, "Because I will have the shortest travel time as I can to get back to them." Tyrn searches my features, and his eyes widen.

"You're not really considering attacking the Pauraque at Opus," he states, his tone pleading for me to say no.

I look out over the snow, clearing all doubts from my mind and simply desiring that I get back to the group. "We will try, whether we can succeed or not. If there's one thing that you'll learn about us, is that Arne taught us not to go down without a really big fight. And I know Rhi and Cici are already preparing, so they're going to need every set of wings and talons they can get."

Narrator

Byhi is, needless to say, infuriated. The Fate Owl has let her down. When she sang his hoots and led her soldiers to follow, her plan had fallen apart. Her soldiers joined with the rebels, and had screeched defiantly, right in front of her. Now they are all paying the price. But that isn't enough. She needs something more. More punishment might satisfy her for the magnitude of treachery they have committed against her rule.

The Pauraque will make her into a feather-duster if she does not succeed. She can just as easily take away the purple robe, golden pin, and silver mask from Byhi and hand it to another owl. But Byhi must prove to her that she is the only one for the job. She has to show the Pauraque that she can have success and that she has more drive, more hunger, than any other owl.

Byhi looks down off her perch. Under her talons is the replica of Argon. Byhi will be queen over all Argon. She can order around every single owl that lives in Argon, even the revered snowies. All of it will be hers. She can do as she pleases, whenever she pleases.

But she has to prove her worth first. And the first step is making sure all her soldiers are in line; which they are not.

She looks over and sees the set of golden tips. Byhi grabs them slowly, and fits them onto her claws. She smiles, her own image gleaming in the oil-polished metal. This will make quite a show.

***

A sea of soldiers lies before her, copper masks shining on top of their heads. Hundreds of eyes give her full attention, but that does not mean that there are friendly gazes. Just a whole lot of hatred. The punishment did nothing to make them respect or be afraid of Byhi; it just made them angrier and more rebellious. That is the tricky thing with punishment. Sometimes it just fuels the fire.

"I am disappointed in your behavior when we faced Arne," Byhi growls to them, her silver mask gleaming in the light, "All of you have failed me. The only reason why you are still living is because of the kindness and understanding of the Pauraque, as well as my plans for you."

From the more intelligent soldiers, alarm bells go off. Something about the statement sends shivers down them. They should've tried to escape right then.

"You will be divided into groups, led by some of my more trusted associates. You will start to find out the weaknesses of each division of Argon, and report back to me with a list. The list must include an estimated population of birds living there, potential threats—this will include leaders of these birds, stronger specimens, or the elders—the best way to invade this division, and its natural defenses," Byhi announces, "There will be four operations, one for each division. Some of you will be in a plan codenamed 'Gold-Mine'. The desert will be the easier task. Or some of you might explore the marsh in operation 'Maximum Density'. Keep in mind that whoever survives the marsh will be highly revered, as no owl has come back yet. Arko Forest will be a large ordeal, and whoever is chosen for the project will be guided into the plan, 'Timber'. And finally, there is the arctic to be dealt with. Operation 'Blindsight' will be our main priority. Know that only the best and the brightest will be picked to work on this project. Best of luck, the results for which operation you are to be placed in will be revealed tomorrow."

Mutters about operation 'Gold-Mine', 'Maximum Density', 'Timber', and 'Blindsight' circulate around the crowd, conspiracy theories already forming. Some soldiers already have in their minds what division their target will be.

Byhi clears her throat.

"I will expect more from you in the future, mind you." She warns. "If not..." Byhi opens her talons quickly, creating sparks and igniting the oil-polished talons in fire. The front line of soldiers unconsciously back up, fear erupting in their hearts. Byhi stares at the soldiers for a moment, the fire resting in her talons. Then Byhi is gone, and the soldiers file out from the cavern, many different thoughts swirling around in their heads. It is finally clear.

Byhi and the Pauraque are going through with their plan to conquer all of Argon.

Byhi walks away from them, heading back to her chambers.

Little does she know that she won't hold another meeting the next night. She'll have much more important things to deal with. Such as rouge snowy owls and traitors. Yes...Byhi will have a lot on her mind tomorrow.

Arne

The full moon's light slowly starts to enter my cell, lighting up the space with its soft blue-silver glow. Tonight I won't just call to the rebels, I will be *with* them.

I fly up and out of the ceiling, bursting into the cool of the night air. I breathe deeply, preparing myself. Slowly, I put pressure on the chains. They creak and stretch just slightly, but then they stop giving. They pull taut once more, the shackles biting into my ankles. I grit my beak. They're giving a lot more resistance then I thought they would.

I pull harder, straining myself. A hear a few sickening cracks, but nothing more. There are no signs of ripping free.

"Well, I can't give up now. Peh, patience is *key*," I mutter, scolding myself for saying such things, "I'm fed up...with being...chained...to a *wall*." I push harder, for all I'm worth. Maybe my calculations were incorrect. I should've waited a few more nights. Walls weaken slowly.

Too *slow!* I think. *I will escape* now.

The shackles threaten to pop my feet clean off, but I tense up, and dig my claws into the earth. A small owl flies up from his cell, a single chain trailing from one of his feet. He looks over and jumps slightly at the sight of me. His mouth drops slightly, and I try and visualize myself.

A three-foot-tall snowy owl straining against double chains, muscles bulging, beak gritted. Fire dancing in her eyes as she gazes into the distance, focusing on breaking free.

Owls, I must be scary.

I spare a glance at him, and I nod. He stares for a moment, and then starts to fly, pulling hard at his iron cuff. I shake my head.

"Get...down...dig your talons...into the ground," I grunt, "It focuses...your efforts." He nods, and worriedly lands onto the ground, obediently copying my technique and trying to break the chain. He's a small owl, and seems to be a Ferruginous pygmy owl. Obviously, just by listening to his name, you know he's pretty small in comparison to me. The only other owl bigger than myself would be the Great grey. And if I know Byhi, she would've probably only used the Bay owl soldiers to escort this little guy.

His chest heaves rapidly as he closes his eyes tightly, pulling and pulling against his chain. I do the same, and finally feel the iron moving against my strength. Or perhaps it was the wall. Either way, I am making progress.

With an ear-splitting metal-pop, it gives way. I stumble and roll quite a few times, the force I had been exerting suddenly pushing against open air. I take a couple breaths, and roll onto my back. The poor little Ferruginous pygmy owl's chains are as thick as toothpicks. I laboriously get up, and with a single snap of my beak, I cut the chain in half. He blinks and looks up at me, amazed at my power.

"Where are the bigger owls held?" I ask him.

"Hall 23, section B, level 1," he answers simply.

"Okay, I'm sorry but I didn't understand a word of what you said. Could you just lead me there instead?"

The little owl bobs his head furiously, and takes off, giddy with the sensation of flight. He was finally free again.

And so am I, I remind myself, chasing after him.

He twists and turns, hugging the edge of the gray wooden walkway. Soon we come upon another set of holes, where dark cells lie below, with rebels waiting for the position of the moonlight to start the Call.

"Here we are," the little owl announces.

"It was just around the corner," I mutter, humiliated. I screech loudly, just as if I was starting the Call, and within a few seconds, an owl from every hole flies out, landing gracefully on the edge. They seemed stunned to see me right here, hovering right in front of them. It is an appropriate reaction.

"It's time to go," I boom, swooping in towards them. I land in front of one of the owls, a Short-eared female, and nod to her. Still moving slowly and trying to compute what is happening, she lifts up her chain. I take it, hook it around my beak, and use a claw to pull. After a few seconds, it breaks, falling to the ground with a heavy *clunk*.

"If you could start helping the others," I begin. There was no need to finish. She nods enthusiastically, and hurriedly wobbles over to one of the owls, trying to get used to not compensating for the weight of the chain anymore.

Within a few minutes, we've snapped all the chains. "I need you to free every single owl, and pass on the order to 'free more owls'. Do the bigger ones first so they can help the smaller species. I have some business to attend to, and I will be back...however, I don't know how much time it might take."

The owls before me nod with understanding. One of the bigger owls of the group steps forward. "Is this the final assault? Are we going to take on the Pauraque?"

I smile with a gleam in my eye. "Yes," I say, with feeling, "This is the day we get back our freedom." The owl nods, smiling as well. Some mischief is going to be created, and Byhi will be up to her ear-tufts in our trouble.

I turn, and take to the skies. I have to find my group. If they're coming, then I need to protect them. They could be caught in the crossfire.

And I swear, if any owl hurts so much as a feather on them, I will deal with them...

...*personally.*

Nyk

"I'll speed ahead and keep Byhi occupied," Intyl promises. I nod, and watch him pick up speed, beating his wings faster and faster. I can see Opus now, and the trees of Arko Forest are starting to disappear around me as I reach the border.

With a sudden rush of wind, it's open air. I've reached the center of Argon.

A few small figures flutter around where the ceilings of the cell-quadrant is, and I hear some metallic snaps. Like chains breaking...

Arne. She's the only one who could ever have the beak-power to break iron chains. But she was shackled with double chains! A chain on each foot. No owl could break that.

Then again, no owl should've broken the *single* chain either, and Arne did.

Sure enough, a snowy white figure takes off from the commotion and heads toward me. Arne grows closer, and I can see her feathers rippling in the wind, her eyes showing that she is set on some goal.

But then those eyes focus on me, and a dark hatred clouds them.

"Oh, no," I mutter. Arne still thinks that I'm her enemy. To her, I work for Byhi. I never had a chance to tell her of my plan. And apparently, she could escape just fine without my help. She had made a plan of her own.

Arne screeches with rage, and slams into me. I'm pushed backwards, and land on a stray tree, gripping a branch before I fall. With some struggle, I manage to perch and watch as Arne lands, tensed and *very* angry.

"You gave up without a fight!" she screams, slamming me into the trunk of the tree. "You fell to Byhi willingly!"

"Yes!" I plead, "Yes, I did! But just hear me out!"

"Never!" Arne screams, "You're a liar, and a traitor, and you're full of owl-pellets! Now you're just Byhi's little pet, who'll do anything for her with a smile on your face!"

"I did it for *you*!" I blurt out. Arne freezes, something she doesn't do often.

I blink a few times, ashamed at the way it sounded. "I...I let Byhi make me into one of her commanders so that I'd have access to the prisoner's cells." I stutter. Arne looks at me curiously, her anger fading. "I wanted to get you out of there," I continue, "I didn't want you to stay there for the rest of your life."

Arne doesn't seem to quite compute this. "You...you cared...about *me*?"

"Yes," I whisper, "The moment I met you I wanted to help you. You were meant to be free." I pause just slightly, adding feeling. "I want you to be happy." Arne stares at me, longingly, seeing my sacrifice. Then she shakes her head, and clears herself of the moment.

Arne punches me in the wing, but it seems partially playful. "Thank you," she says, "But I have it under control."

"How..." I ask, "How did you break those chains?" Arne smiles, being herself again.

"Same way I did the last ones," she says simply, and then she takes off.

"Where are you going?" I call.

"To find my group," she answers, her voice full of power and determination. And promise. Promise of payback.

Then she's gone.

***

I wander 'round the halls, breathless. "Intyl?" I call. "Intyl?" I turn a corner that leads to Byhi's chamber and walk into a brigade of owl soldiers. Byhi and Intyl stand at the front.

"Hello, Nyk," Byhi says, and edge to her voice. I quickly glance at Intyl, and realize his demeanor's changed.

"Oh yes," Byhi coos, "You're little friend Intyl was with me after all. Such a loyal little guy, isn't he? He can find out anything."

"No," I say, backing up, "No, no no no." My voice increases with volume as swells of panic rise within me like tidal waves. *Intyl betrayed me. He was never a rebel. He lied. He's Byhi's pet, through and through. He's told her everything, and now Byhi knows that I'm the traitor.*

And then a thought. *Arne. Oh Arne, run!*

I turn, and try and escape, but then they're upon me.

Cici

There's a white owl in the distance.

"Arne?" I call out. Rhi sees the figure too, and we fly faster, heading towards it.

"Cici?" The snowy owl asks. Rhi and I look at each other simultaneously, eyes brightening. It's always good to have Arne with you when you're going to battle.

"Arne!" we shout. She's close enough to see the details, and it looks like her wing has healed. Her ankles, however, are in rough shape. It appears as if she broke some chains and the cuffs dug into her skin.

Arne impacts us hard, momentarily hugging us. We let go, and then we're all hovering, smiles on our faces.

"You made it out!" I say, smiling. Arne seems hesitant.

"Yes," she replies, but cocks her head to the side as she sees a snowflake on my shoulder. "Where have you been?"

"To your homeland," Rhi answers, "We tried to rally the rest of the snowy owls." Arne shakes her head solemnly.

"Tyrn is the only one who would accept your story. If he couldn't rally them, then practically no one could,"

"Maybe Ayia could," I try hopefully. Arne seems confused.

"Who?"

"Ayia," I repeat. Arne finally nods, some memories dawning on her.

"Yes, the skeptical one. Typical snowy owl."

"She helped us get through the blizzard and back to Arko Forest," Rhi explains.

"Most interesting," Arne hurriedly says, "But you must go." I search Arne's features, trying to pick out what could be worrying her so much.

"What are you not telling us?" I ask. Arne sighs.

"There's a rebellion going on, and I don't want you two in the middle of it," she pleads.

"I'm not an owlet anymore! And Rhi here wants to finally get back at the owls that worked her so hard for all those years!" I shout. Arne shakes her head, and grows firm.

"I cannot let you get caught in the crossfire," she says.

"Too bad," I persist, flying past Arne, "I'm going."

I leave Arne, approaching Opus. There seems to be some commotion going on. Several owls fight soldiers, more and more fighters from both sides pouring into the skies.

"Time for some payback," Rhi growls, now flying beside me. Arne comes from the rear, eventually flying ahead of us.

"Please be careful," she says, and then we're all in the fray.

"For Theo," I growl, and start slashing at the soldiers. The owls that fight alongside me must be some freed rebel prisoners, because they screech and claw with as much hatred and motivation as I do.

I try and fight the Great greys, but they knock me aside like ragdolls. Eventually some-bird bumps into me from behind, and I whip around. An Eastern screech owl with a bronze battle-mask stares back at me, and we engage in combat.

This must be the owl that got picked to be a soldier with Arne. He sure does seem like a soldier to me.

"Why are you fighting for the wrong side," I ask between slashes. The owl seems surprised, but continues parrying and jabbing nevertheless.

"I am fighting for the side I was Recruited for," he answers simply.

"Why aren't you fighting with the rebels," I press. His eyes dart around, as if he were fighting a mental battle. But he finally makes up his mind, looking me in the eye.

"You do what you have to in order to survive," he tells me.

Kari

Tyrn and I watch the battle ahead of us, examining both sides. The rebels against the soldiers.

"You're really going to help?" I ask, trying to confirm whether he's going to stay or not. Tyrn sighs, but eventually nods, giving in.

"Yeah," he says, "I guess I am." His eyes become unfocused as he sees Arne.

"Is that really..." he trails off.

"We were telling the truth," I say, shrugging my shoulders. Well, I shrugged them as best as I could since we were still flying.

Some soldiers spot us, and change their course to meet us.

"We've got company," I mutter. Tyrn nods, loosening his claws, ready to strike.

When we collide, I instantly know that this will be all that I can handle. No big leaders to fight or big roles for me to play. I get to hold off the soldiers while everyone else is in the spotlight, taking down Byhi or the Pauraque or something.

It might be safer, my optimistic side says.

I can just see the realistic side of me shaking its head...

...soldiers can be just as deadly.

Narrator

Owl fought owl. The constant scraping of talons on metal masks and the ripping of feathers fills the air, the sounds of battle echoing in every owl's ears.

The rebels are untrained, but their hatred fuels a lot of their movements and compensates. The soldiers just keep coming though. No one but Byhi or the Pauraque knew the true numbers of their army. Hundreds and hundreds of owls with copper masks pour out from Opus, each one giving their own battle cry.

The rebels are being overwhelmed. Soldiers are starting to close in. Obviously, it is a great relief when Kari and Tyrn enter the fight, making Cici, Rhi, and Arne all fight a little harder, glad that she made it out.

Kari manages to fight alongside Cici, helping her take on a Short-eared owl. "How'd you get out of there?" Cici asks. Kari slashes, and watches the soldier fall.

"Tyrn," she answers simply. As if on cue, Tyrn breaks into the fray, scaring the soldiers a little. After all, the only snowies around should've been Nyk and Arne.

Tyrn gravitates toward Arne, who is sparring with a Great grey.

"Hey Arne," Tyrn breathes. Arne spares a glance, and smiles, radiating honest joy. Two old friends reunited.

"Tyrn," Arne exclaims, giving a final blow to the Great grey so that she can get a good look at Tyrn. Tyrn spots the damage on Arne's ankles from the chains, and Arne follows his gaze, cracking a grin.

"I broke some chains today," Arne says, whipping around and catching a Short-eared—who had tried to stealthily sneak up on her—with a back-hand blow.

"Go Snowy Ghosts!" The two snowies say simultaneously, yelling the battle cry as if they were cheering for a favorite football team.

But Arne falters for a moment, a hole inside her becoming clear. She looks to the sky, and back to Opus. "Where's Nyk?" she breathes. She dismisses the thought and knows he'll be alright, and continues fighting ever harder.

But despite everyone's efforts, the soldiers just kept coming. More and more mass around them, hundreds of them turning into a swarm that look to be a thousand. A battle of major proportions.

On the horizon, a white wisp of fog rolls in, like an arising storm. The rebels and soldiers dismiss it as simply a front from Dilecta Arctic, but Arne, Tyrn, Cici, Rhi and Kari know better. They've been to the arctic, and can tell a storm of snow from a band of owls.

Of course, as the front grows closer and does not dissipate, the soldiers grow uneasy. They have seen Nyk and Arne before, and worry what could happen if there were dozens of them.

Those soldiers are right to be worried.

Around thirty snowies glide in, their auras of experience and power washing over the soldiers like the drowning sea. Reinforcements have arrived.

In the front of the band is a large snowy owl, led by a small, brown owl. "Nara!" Cici yells, finishing off another Short-eared owl. There is no doubt that her sister is leading the attack.

And sure enough, Nara is that small brown Burrowing owl at the front of the taskforce. Ayia has rallied her comrades, and now her actions might turn the tide of the rebellion.

The gang of snowy owls casts a shadow on the soldiers, and they hover for a split second, making every soldiers' heart race rapidly.

Then they descend, screeching something immensely powerful. Imagine Arne's screech times thirty and that's what the soldiers hear. Suffice to say, it is loud. And terrifying.

The snowy owls roll in and fight like a mini blizzard. The ranks of the soldiers are quickly thrown into chaos, and the rebel owls cheer. Maybe they have a chance after all.

Rhi

Nara fights with all she has, making her way to her sister. When I saw her swoop in, it was like a weight was lifted. I can't imagine what Cici must be feeling, to have her sister come back from the depths of a snowstorm.

But I have problems of my own, and couldn't enjoy the moment. A single loud, blurry whistle cuts through the noise. "purr-WHEE-eer".

I've only heard stories about it. About *her*. They say the Pauraque is "the bird in the shadows" and that she's never been seen before. The ones who claim to know all about her say she has an uncanny resemblance to a rattlesnake. I think it's fitting, since she hisses a lot, and the words she speaks and the things she does is just as venomous.

A single bird flies above the battle; three short wing beats then rest, three short wing beats then rest...

I quickly slip past my opponent and break through the battle. The bird turns, and a bunch of things hit me at once.

When the owls said the Pauraque had "an uncanny resemblance to a rattlesnake," they were spot on. The Pauraque is a slightly stout bird, and very short compared to me. She's around eleven inches long, and looks to be in the night-jar family. But the thing that strikes me the most is the coloration of her feathers. They're designed to look like a rattlesnake's scales as he's coiled, and I would've very much believed she was reptilian had she not been hovering in mid-flight. Her brown eyes lock with mine, and they look like a cauldron of poisonous, boiling sludge. It seems as though, even if she was in a good mood, the color of her eyes would still be, at best, looking like freezer-burned fudge.

Fear grips me hard, but I fight it away. "YOU!" I shriek, coming at her. I slash but she dodges, and continues to evade my attacks. Rage fills my tiny frame. This is the bird that ordered that I should work for the rest of my life, that I should be taken away from my family. My life was *ruined* because of her!

I manage to rake a talon on one of her wings, and I feel satisfied. But it disappears. *You deserve much more than that.*

Finally, she flees. I chase after her, just burning with anger inside. *You will not run away. You will face the consequences for what you've done.*

The Pauraque is almost to Arko Forest. She uses that pattern, three wing beats then glide, and speeds through the air. I gain speed, but she enters the forest-line, and takes one last glance back at me. Those brown eyes stare at me, and an invisible smile of triumph rests on her beak. *Just wait*, she seems to say, *I will be back for you.*

Kari

A Great grey approaches me, and I'm separated from Cici. No other rebels can lend me a talon.

So I try and take him on myself. His immense power rivals that of Arne's and obviously I am no match for some-owl like Arne. Eventually, I tire, and my dodges grow sluggish. He goes to slash, and time slows down, his claws starting to press against my neck, slowly traveling through the feathers.

A supernaturally white figure bursts from the air, and parries his strike. With a single blow he pushes the Great grey owl away, where he is swallowed by the disorganized fray of battle. The owl turns to me, and I gasp. He smiles.

"You chose the right side, Kari," he says. Time becomes real again, and then he's gone. The Destiny Owl disappears, as if he was never here.

Chapter 10: Love Hurts

Arne

It feels good to have my brethren here. Tyrn and Ayia managed to convince the rest of the Snowy Ghosts to help the rebels.

The soldiers are thinning out. We're winning.

But something is nagging me. Like something horrible is happening. Nyk. Where is he? His name swirls in my thoughts. *Nyk. Where is Nyk?*

I try and leave the battle, but a Great grey catches me. He looks me in the eye. "Oh no you're not," he growls, and slashes. Tyrn jumps in front, and engages the Great grey.

"Go!" Tyrn shouts to me. "Go finish whatever you were doing." I nod in appreciation, and slip away, flying towards Opus, towards my prison.

***

I land softly, and peer down the hall. There has been no sign of Byhi in the battle. There's no telling who could be here.

I start down the hall, cautiously scouting in every room as I make my way, looking for any signs of Byhi or the Pauraque. I hear scraping down the hall, and whispers. I slow my pace, inching towards the room. The whispers grow louder. Someone's talking. "Nyk?" I ask. I continue inching forward, and the whispers grow louder, owls talking. "Nyk?" I ask again. Everything stops, and all of Opus falls silent.

Something's wrong.

I approach the room, and take a deep breath. Nyk isn't answering, and Byhi was missing from battle. If Nyk has been captured...no, I shall free him. We will have our freedom together. I will wait on him just as he promised to me.

I whip around into the room, and see my old enemy. Byhi freezes in shock, eyes wide beneath her silver battle mask. Her richly purple robe flutters in the breeze, and I see a large Great grey next to her, staring me down. He wears no mask, and is abnormally big. He has to stand around four feet tall.

A couple Short-eared owls stand guard as two other Great greys hold up a battered owl. The owl's feathers are pure white, ruffled in the slight breeze. A fallen bronze mask gently spins on the floor, recently fallen. The owl lifts his eyes, and they lock with mine. The utter sense of defeat and a determined fire burned down to ashes strikes me hard, and I choke on the feeling of it. Nyk holds my gaze, bruised, beaten, and alone. I want to break down and cry, to scream at him "You are not alone! I will get you out of here!" But it would seem foolish. I am stronger than that. I instead turn to Byhi once more, and my emotions burn down to a single feeling. Rage.

"What have you done to him?" I scream at her. Byhi shakes herself of shock, and regains her aura of power. She addresses me coolly, as if nothing was wrong.

"Just what he deserves," she coos. She steps closer to Nyk and uses a claw to lift up his chin, tracing his neck with a claw. "What a little traitor," she murmurs, "You looked me in the eye and said you'd serve me till the end of your days. And you left me for Arne. You took one look at Arne and fell for her. Intyl stayed faithful. He knows what side is strong."
"What are you talking about," I ask nervously, stepping

closer. Byhi continues her one-sided conversation with Nyk, ignoring me.

"Yes, I promised you power, I promised you a future with me, to be in control. You would never go to the Under-Hollows again. You'd be safe with me. But you had to go and get attached to Arne, and then you turned on me, just like that. You traitorous little snake. You played me, and now you and Arne will pay the ultimate price." I start approaching Byhi now, growing more nervous by the second. Price? What price? What must we pay?

Byhi turns to me, her eyes full of hatred of my very existence. "You took him from me!" she screams, "If I cannot have him at my side, then no one will! Especially not you!" My heart starts racing. Byhi is becoming hysterical. When your enemy doesn't think logically anymore you have a right to be afraid. Because logic leaves them and they just start lashing out, doing things that don't make sense but are still horrifically evil.

And now that I care, that I have owls that I love and want to protect, she can hurt me badly without even touching me. And she has Nyk right now. She can do anything to Nyk. Anything she pleases.

Byhi screeches loudly, her voice full of hatred, of longing, of death from a broken heart. She steps toward Nyk, and grabs a silver piece of metal, gripping it hard in her claws, tears brimming her eyes. The silver dagger glitters in the moonlight softly, knowing its place. Byhi guides it, aiming it for Nyk's heart.

"No!" I scream, hurling myself towards her. The Great grey tries to stop me, but I use the force of my momentum to push him out of my way. As the silver dagger nears Nyk, I grab it forcefully, taking it out of Byhi's claws. I land hard, and I grip the dagger tightly by the middle, its blade sinking into my skin. It hurts to hold it, but I grit my beak and stare Byhi in the eye.

"You will not take him away from me," I growl, clenching the dagger even tighter. I don't care if it hurts. Love hurts.

Byhi screeches, more defeated than ever. She pounces on me, but I deflect, and easily pin her down. She has nothing, but I have *everything* to fight for.

"Cyndern!" Byhi calls. The Great grey immediately lifts me from Byhi, and throws me against the wall of the cavern. Byhi slips away, disappearing without a sound like some cursed shadow.

I face the Great grey, and realize he was the same one who held Cici for my capture. Cyndern interprets my gaze, and smiles cruelly. "Ah, you recognize me."

"Let the Fate Owl take you," I growl. Cyndern laughs, looking down on me with his immense height. His eyes sparkle with bloodlust.

"Who was your little friend again? Cici? And this is your lover? Nyk?" Cyndern looks over at Nyk, but I screech loudly, reverting his attention back to me.

"You leave them out of this!" I screech. Cyndern looks at me curiously, smiling.

"Oh, but I think they have everything to do with this, you see, Nyk betrayed Byhi because he cared about you," Cyndern stares at Nyk with disgust and intrigue, and continues his story, "He even tried to get Intyl into the rebellion. But Intyl was as true to Byhi as I am, and we did not stand for his rebellion. Because if there is one thing we have learned about you, is that you have changed. You care, and that is weakness. You should have never left the arctic."

He starts to move closer to Nyk, but I take flight and slash at his neck feathers. His eyes immediately snap to me, and I hover there, my hatred turning into fuel for my protection of Nyk. "You shall not touch him," I growl, and we engage in battle.

It should have been over in a matter of seconds. Cyndern should have easily won by size. But I wasn't an ordinary Snowy owl. Everything didn't boil down to the advantage of size. He didn't have a very strong motive, but I did. I had Nyk.

We slash and parry, ripping feathers from each other's bodies. After a few blows, Cyndern simply crashes into me, crushing me with his immense size. The breath is knocked out of my lungs, and darkness rushes to claim my vision. I hear Nyk scream my name, and for a moment, I lose focus.

Nyk throws himself at Cyndern, but he is in bad shape, and Cyndern simply flicks him off his shoulder, sending him sailing across the room. However, in those few seconds, he saved my life. It gives me time to rally, and Cyndern is slightly distracted, just for a few seconds.

It isn't much, but every second counts.

With a screech, I counter-attack Cyndern, drawing his attention back to me. "You try to take everything from me!" I screech, parrying potentially fatal blows and attacking with moves of my own, "You tried to take Cici. You tried to take my freedom. Now you want to claim Nyk!" Cyndern laughs, dark power echoing through the chamber.

"You speak as though the battle has not already been lost," Cyndern says.

I glance over, and see Nyk struggling back to his feet, so broken yet so strong and unbeatable. He meets my eyes, and for a moment I'm completely calm. "You promised," I say aloud, more to Nyk than to Cyndern, "That if I am condemned to this place, you would stay by my side, you would wait for me till we gained our freedom. I, in turn, make this promise."

"What a lovely confession," Cyndern grunts, trying to stop my advance.

"So," I continue, "I'll make this quick so we won't have long to wait." I lock eyes with Cyndern, and I see uncertainty flicker in his eyes as he notices my serenity. I take a deep breath, and I see my life flash before my eyes. The winter wolf. My time in the arctic. Cici and Nara. Kari. Theo. Rikki and Celfina. Rhi. Byhi. Nyk.

Nyk.

With a final screech, I crash into Cyndern, knocking him off balance. I drive myself into him, and with immense force he crashes into the wall, dirt and rock and debris crumbling to dust around us. Cyndern falls into open air, myself along with him, spiraling down once more. I remember my spirals with Rikki and Celfina, and learn from it. I see what I can do to save myself. I catch a draft, and hover above, watching Cyndern plummet. Theo, you've saved my life. A second time.

I fly back inside the cavern, touching down and staring at Nyk. We look at each other for a good long moment, then Nyk breaks the silence.

"You...are amazing," he says, smiling. I smile softly in response. I open my beak to say something to him, trying to think of something meaningful, when I hear an odd bird call pierce the battle. I whip my head around, peering out into the skies.

"We need to get back," Nyk says. I look at him, up and down.

"You can't. Wait here," I order. Nyk shakes his head.

"I'm not that bad. I'll do my part, but I promise I won't over-exert myself,"

I grit my beak for a moment, then finally nod, and launch myself off the ledge, heading towards the battle once more.

Chapter 11: The Final Plays

Arne

A brown streak of a bird flies past, Rhi in hot pursuit. It must be the Pauraque, the way Rhi's eyes burn with hatred. The Pauraque must have been the bird I had heard. I try and pull away to help, but three Great greys occupy my attention.

The flow of the soldiers has stopped completely. Actually, a lot of them are fleeing now. The Twin Wings screech once and all the soldiers try and follow them as they retreat into the distance towards Worte Marsh.

The snowy owls give chase, and I see a Eurasian Eagle owl trying to escape. Her silver mask glitters in the moonlight.

"Byhi!" I shout, "You're not going anywhere!" Byhi looks at me, and this time, there is no hidden plan to save her, no fallout plot that will keep her from the consequences. She quickly turns and flies for all she's worth, and I go after her, beating my wings hard to gain speed and catch up with her.

Everything she's done to me quickly flashes through my mind. The first assault, when she damaged my wing. Then how she imprisoned me here, making me endure the training, trying to make Nyk into a soldier, ruining so many owls' lives. She wanted to kill Nyk. She said that if she couldn't have him no one could. She will not get away this time. Not this time.

It isn't hard to catch up with her. In her desperation she just can't get the power-stroke. I latch onto her back and swing her around. She tries to fight, but I quickly subdue her. I look into her eyes. They're full of fear.

"You should be afraid," I growl. My grip on her claws grows tighter and she whimpers. "What you did to those owls is unforgivable." My emotions try and take hold of me, and I grip Byhi harder. "What you did to me and Nyk is unforgivable!"

Byhi's eyes cloud. "Yes, and so is this." She jerks free and slashes a talon across my beak. I screech loudly, and she tries to escape. But I quickly fly towards her and, with a single blow, send her spiraling to the rocky ground below. Some feathers float up and dance in her wake, just like I did when she sent me down to Arko below. The difference was...she isn't going to get up from that one.

I fly back to the battle scene, and catch a glimpse of Intyl scurrying away, managing to catch up with the disappearing migration of soldiers. And...next to him...an over-sized Great grey.

Cyndern stares at me one last time, his expression cold and unmoving. Then he breaks his gaze and follows Intyl in retreat, disappearing from sight.

My group and a couple of the Snowy Ghosts now hover near Opus, watching me approach them. "Byhi has been dealt with," I announce, and nods ripple all around.

"The Pauraque escaped," Rhi mutters angrily, "She slipped away."

"So did Intyl, and Cyndern," I confirm. Ayia keeps looking down, quiet. Ayia and Nyk are the only ones here besides my group

"Where's Tyrn? And where are the rest of the Snowy Ghosts?" I ask. From Ayia's expression I know exactly what happened as soon as I asked the question.

"He's gone," she whispers. She takes a moment, and then continues. "A few others from the Snowy Ghosts fell as well."

"Most of them just got a head start back to the arctic though," Nyk clarifies.

I sigh. "There are a lot of loose ends to be dealt with. The Pauraque, the Twin Wings, Cyndern and Intyl are still out there, along with quite a few of their army..."

"Wait, who's Cyndern?" Nara asks.

I suppress a wave of rage at the sound of his name. "He's the Great grey who tried to kill Cici. He almost killed me and Nyk, too." Nara's eyes cloud with hatred, but she takes a deep breath. Her mini-episode draws her attention away from the potential explanation of my battle with Cyndern. I still have unsorted emotions. It's best not to dredge them up quite yet.

"The rebels have dispersed and have gone home, I assume?" I ask, interrupting Nara's brooding.

"Yes," Rhi answers. I turn to my group alone, wanting to smile. Cici, Nara, Kari and now Rhi too. They all made it out.

"What do you want to do now?" I ask quietly. We know what their choices are; we either stick together and hunt down the rest of the Pauraque's organization or go our separate ways.

"I'm going to take care of those loose ends," Cici says boldly, puffing out her chest as if she were preparing for something big. And she was. Nara nods approvingly, and Rhi smiles in agreement, a gleam in her eye.

"Then I'm coming with you," I whisper softly. Cici smiles genuinely, something that I fear will become a rare occasion.

"We're going to search for Theo while we're at it though, right?" Cici asks, looking like her old self again. I smile, a sad tint to it, and nod my head.

"Um," Nyk says, trying to get our attention, "Can uh...can I...what I mean is..." I roll my eyes.

"Yes?" I prompt quietly. Nyk laughs once, but finally manages to say it.

"Can I join?"

There is momentary silence. It's appropriate, as no one but me knows what he's been through and whether he's trustworthy or not. "Of course," I say softly.

"So," I introduce, "This is Nyk. Nyk, there's Cici and Nara, Kari, and Rhi. You've now met the group."

"I've busted my tail feathers rounding up the Snowy Ghosts," Ayia starts to complain. Kari takes her turn, and bursts out laughing.

"Yes yes, you're in. We're all one big, happy family now. But can we move on? I'm tired, and I haven't felt my favorite perch underneath my talons in months," Kari complains.

"Alright," I give in, "One night." Laughing, Kari, Nara, Cici and Rhi start to depart. Ayia pauses, looking up at the sky.

"Tyrn's last words were, 'The stars are out tonight,'" she whispers. She blinks back tears and joins the others.

My new-and-improved group starts to fly in the direction of Arko Forest, when I see that Nyk isn't moving to join them. "What is it?" I ask softly, hovering beside him.

"Thank you," he says. I blink once in surprise.

"There's no need, we're..."

"For being there for me," Nyk explains, "For giving me something to look up to. None of us could've done this without you." I smile slightly.

"And thank you," I say in return, "For staying true and not giving in to Byhi. You stood up against all odds. You held on for me." I'd never said something so emotional before, but it felt good telling Nyk about what he did.

I nudge his shoulder. "Now come on, let's get some rest." We glide down to catch up with the others, gazing up at a black-and-blue night, moonlight shining on our backs. We soar into the distance under starry skies.

End Note

I want to use this book to reach out to you, the reader. As an author I am often asked about my story's theme, and I am asked in effect to distill my story into a single message. But I can't, honestly. This is a story, with no one purpose but to share this tale with the world. But, like every good life story, there *are* things that you can learn from. There are important themes to be noticed from this book.

Each character had something they learned or grew into. So, may I have your attention for a short time to show you these things? Thank you.

Arne is the main character of this story, and I believe she also might be my favorite. The main transformation she experienced was love. She used to be a cold and distant owl, suspicious and untrusting. When she woke up inside the hollow for the first time is a good example of this. But in the end she learned to trust, and saw herself becoming more and more willing to sacrifice her freedom for the freedom of others. Because there's no shame in caring. There's no shame in trusting.

Nyk did come in later in the book, but he was important. He showed loyalty. He taught Arne to love, and even though it broke his heart to go undercover to work for Byhi he stayed true to her. Loyalty is an honorable quality, but it takes strength in order to have it.

Then again, Intyl showed us the other side of loyalty. *Intyl*, the owl with all the *Intel*. He argued he was working for the Pauraque in order to survive, but if that was true he would've picked whatever side was winning at the time. Loyalty is only worth something if it's for the right side.

Rikki and Celfina revealed to us that in the world of power and corruption, anyone can be replaced. As well as the fact that you can lose yourself in the world of evil, and once you're gone, you're willing to do anything to bring down your enemy, even if it's the cost of your own life.

Rhi can tell us that it doesn't matter how hard you've been knocked down, or how bad you've been treated. You can get back up again and have just as much fire if not more than ever before. You can bend from years of wear and tear, but you'll never break if you keep faith.

Cici is the little owl that would trust anyone, would believe in anyone. But when Theo was lost, she saw that not everyone is good and caring, not everyone is as happy and compassionate as she was. She saw that there was evil. And she learned how to fight it.

Nara wanted to protect her sister more than anything. But she didn't pay attention to her needs and aches. She didn't get her sister's kind nature so she couldn't help Cici when she needed her most. But she too learned, and grew wise, and finally realized how to help her sister because she understood her. She finally opened up.

Little Theo, his legacy showed us that even if one dies, if one is lost in a worthy cause, hundreds more will follow him and rise up to quell the challenge. He was an inspiration to them all. And even I miss him.

Tyrn, he was the owl who *turned* the tide of the war. Without his help in persuading the snowy owls, all the rebels would have been slaughtered under the claws of the Pauraque's soldiers. But he showed us that in war not everyone will make it out, that not every lives to see another day.

Kari, she was almost too careful and unsure. She couldn't decide anything because she was afraid to take risks. But she had to adapt, she had to be able to take risks otherwise the Pauraque would win. It's okay to take risks.

The Twin Wings might have cared slightly about the little owls in the organization, but they were corrupted. They thought that their word was law, and whoever dishonored or defied it was unworthy and should be eliminated. They were played by the Fate Owl. *Pyre*, the owl of *power*. *Ruole*, the owl who *ruled out* the weak.

Cyndern, he was an imposing figure designed to create fear. *Cyndern*, he would burn the world to *cinders* if fear was allowed to ignite. He was cold and twisted, and I don't think that we've seen the last of him.

And ah, the Pauraque. The mastermind behind it all. She would create games, building organizations filled with prestigious leaders that were her puppets on strings. Then she'd play them, play with the world, like it was her entertainment. And every game she lost, she'd walk away, free, already planning the next game.

And the next game is about to begin.

Acknowledgements

I have many people to thank, for I could have never done this alone. I'd like to thank my mom and my dad for their continuous support, and how they helped push me into not only writing, but editing, this story for publishing. I'd like to thank the WUPIS Club for their council and ideas, for being the best group of friends to me ever! A special thanks to Kiersten, Sarah, Megan, and Christina for their editing! Also like to thank my grandmother, Karen Porter, for going through this whole thing and giving me the little things I missed. And I can't forget Mrs. Shori, a fellow writer who edited my book and read my story. I know there was a lot of work to be done, and you took the challenge undaunted. Thank you all for your support and attention, your inspiration and contributions!

And, of course, I thank my Aunt Sandy (as well as the rest of the Bruce family) for being a spectacular inspiration for my writing!

Behind the Scenes and Encouragement

This novel was written in a single month. Yes, it's true. Through the program NaNoWriMo, I wrote over 52,000 words at the age of 12 years old. I edited it, with the help of friends and family, for about seven months. I published it when I was 13, so to all the young writers out there it is very well possible to get your book published at an early age. I firmly encourage everyone to read as many books as possible in order to better yourself as writer. And once you're ready to commit, participate in NaNoWriMo for the publishing offer you've been waiting for.

IMPORTANT: The cover for this novel is under a Creative Commons Attribution-Share Alike 2.0 Generic license. The background and Snowy owl is attributed to Erin Kohlenberg. The Eurasian Eagle owl is attributed to Peter Trimming.

About the Author

Hannah O'Neal currently resides with her wonderful family in Florida, where she is working on the sequel to this novel and many other stories. You can find her on Figment.com where she currently posts some of her shorter works. This is her first published novel.

Made in the USA
Lexington, KY
04 July 2013